CHABLIS: AVENGING ANGEL
FOR
THE FORGOTTEN
IN
THE CITY OF LOST HOPE

By
Wayne Frye

The Author

Wayne Frye's Aaron Adams series has been popular among Canadian mystery lovers since first appearing in 2005. He provides satirical political commentary to many Canadian newspapers, and his books on politics have created a great deal of controversy. He has written marketing/ advertising textbooks, been a successful U.S. university hockey coach, professor, university president and served as a marketing consultant to hockey teams and motion picture companies. He has been cited for his work with inner-city gang children in the Los Angeles area and been active in the anti-globalization movement. He became a Canadian citizen in 2003 and lives at his beloved Bay View Chateau in Ladysmith, Vancouver Island, British Columbia.

Other Books by Wayne Frye

Hockey Mania and the Mystery of Nancy Running Elk
Something Evil in the Darkness at Hopkins House
How Hockey Saved a Jew From the Holocaust:
The Rudi Ball Story
The Catastrophic Calamities of a Village Idiot
Fighting for Justice in the Land of Hypocrisy
Guide to Alternative Education (13 Editions)
Cataclysmic Dreams in Black and White
Introduction to Advertising
Marketing Plan Work Book
Public Relations Workbook
Advertising Lab Manual
Promotions Workbook
Advertising Design
Fall From Apocalypse
Armageddon Now
Worth
When Jesus Came to Jersey as the Son of Thunder
The Girl Who Danced with the Demons of Darkness
The Girl Who Motivated Murder Most Foul
The Girl Who Said Goodbye for the Last Time
Canadian Angels of Mercy – Nurses in Times of Peril
Points of Rebellion: Aboriginals Who Fought for Justice

Chablis: Avenging Angel for the Forgotten
In the City of Lost Hope

TABLE OF CONTENTS

Chablis: Avenging Angel for the Forgotten
In the City of Lost Hope

TO:

Christine, the sweet little woman in a far away
land who reached out with compassion to an old
man floundering in the wasteland
of blocked creativity.

And, of course, to my dear Lynton who
provided the finishing touches of alluring elegance
and comeliness that made it possible to bring
vibrancy to the project. What a privilege it is to
just be able to gaze upon that wonderful smile that
shines a beacon of light into the darkness. She is
the joyous muse who lifts the heavy heart.

JWF

ISBN: 978-0-9879728-7-3

Fireside Books – Victoria, British Columbia/Port Angeles, Washington
Peninsula Publishing Consortium

PROLOGUE
I HAVE SUCKED BIGGER LOLLIPOPS

Chablis Louise Chavez looked at police Lieutenant Armand Carlton with her dark brown eyes sparkling with that usual "I don't give a damn attitude" that seemed to bore a hole right through you and penetrate your soul. "You call me a bitch and think that insults me. Hell that is a compliment. That means you look at me as a woman, and I am more woman than any man in this police department can handle."

And what a woman she was. Standing 5 feet 6 inches in her 3 inch heels, her magnificent, perfectly formed perky nipples jutting out like two small mountain peaks, her tight-fitting blouse hugging her midriff just enough to show the taunt, rippling abs that pushed at the garment with each breath she took, her jeans forming a sensuous curve around her hips and those long lithe legs leading down to her gorgeous feet and the perfectly pedicured toenails with bright red nail polish glistening in the pale light of the squad room made her look like dynamite that might explode any minute.

Lieutenant Carlton, clinching his right fist, leaned forward over his desk and said, "I don't need this Chablis. You caused enough trouble around here when you were gumshoeing with Aaron Adams. We were glad when you turned in your P.I. licence and got married. We have the right man. We know it, because every piece of evidence points to Deluca. So, he is your husband. So what, that does not make him something special. First, in my book, that makes him a goddamn queer. You are wrong. I don't see you as a woman. I see you as an abomination, a freak of nature. You should find a hole and crawl in it, pull the earth over you and hide your despicable self from the world. Your kind is ruining the moral fibre of this country. Get the hell out of my office, and do us all a favour – get the hell out of New York City."

Chablis smiled the smile with all those glistening, gleaming white teeth showing, sparkling in the dully dim-lit squad room as Carlton and three other detectives all had smirks on their faces.

Taking a deep breath and sighing, Chablis, in her soft melodic voice, said, "Listen you son-of-a-bitch, I know what all four of you homophobic bastards are thinking. You all look at me and get a tingle between your legs, because I am more beautiful than any woman any of you has ever been with. You cover-up your desires by berating that which you are too stupid to understand. I may have different equipment between my legs, but I am more woman than any one of you can handle. You are ashamed to admit it, but I know all of you would love to have me wrap my gorgeous puffy lips around those puny things between your legs that you think makes you men."

Then she turned around, and purposely accentuated the sway of her hips to titillate them with her voluptuous posterior as she walked provocatively toward the door, and looking back over her right shoulder, said, "I have sucked bigger lollipops than what you bastards have to offer."

CHAPTER 1
SO EASILY MANIPULATED

Chablis Louise Chavez came to a world of heartache and pain as Pedro Manual Diego Rivera in a small northern Mexico village near the U.S. border with Texas. Her poor, humble parents simply could not deal with the malady with which she was afflicted. Because of their ignorance, when Pedro (nee: Chablis) was only 3, they could not understand why she was always playing with the girls in the village and wanting dolls for presents.

This led to great frustration for these humble peasant parents, because they had no comprehension of gender dysphoria and simply thought they were stuck with an abomination of nature. They did not understand that Chablis felt that her body did not match who she was on the inside. Though she was too young to understand, Chablis at the age of three, started wearing little girl's clothing and insisted she be called Chablis rather than Pedro.

There was a great deal of finger pointing and derisive ridicule from the people of the village. Of course, typical of religion, the village priest said that Pedro was inhabited by an evil demon that was trying to confuse him. Yet, this strong-willed little girl was not confused at all. Although she did not know the scientific reasons, she fully understood that she was a little girl in a little boy's body, and she sat out to do something about it.

By the time she was 12, Chablis had found a source for hormones to make her more feminine, and although the people of the village continued to ridicule her, she noticed that boys and even grown men were beginning to take notice of her feminine charms, and she was not above using them to get what she wanted.

On a school field trip to Mexico City, while visiting the university library, Chablis managed to slip off to a section that had books about gender identity. She spent the day pouring over books describing her condition, and it was then that she decided it was time to stop accepting ridicule from people whom she would henceforth refer to as "dumb fanatical buffoons of bigotry."

When Chablis was 13 years old, she was walking through the village when a man she had known since childhood approached her and said, "I bet you have little titties don't you Chablis?"

Chablis was aware of her appeal to men and she batted her eyes and said, "Yeah, I have them, but a dirty old man like you will never see them."

Frightened that she might reveal his question to her parents, he said, "You better keep your mouth shut about this boy, or you will regret it."

Chablis smiled and said, "First, I am not a boy. I am a girl. Second, you want me to keep my mouth shut, because you are an old pervert who should be thrown out of the village. OK, I will keep my mouth shut, but I intend to get out of this bigoted place when I am 16. Give me 100 pesos a month, and I will keep my mouth shut. That is the price. Pay up you old pervert, or I will expose your lechery to everybody in the village, especially the village priest. Of course, he would like to play with my tits, too. He has already propositioned me. Maybe the two of you should get together and compare notes. You are both perverts, so maybe you two would hit it off and start doing each other."

Even at 13, Chablis was a girl who refused to accept indignities. She was not afraid to stand up for her rights and that was particularly galling to all who dared confront her. Many villagers would find out the hard way that she was not one with whom you could trifle.

By the time she was 14, all the boys and many of the girls in school took delight in tantalizing her. Yet, when the boys were alone with her, they would make indecent proposals, asking for that which all men so ardently desire. Chablis, by now, aware that she could get almost anything she wanted by using her oral talents, was not above using them to obtain what she desired. She saw no shame in it. In fact, to her, the shame was in the hypocrisy of those who used her for their satisfaction, then acted holier than thou at Sunday mass. She really enjoyed giving them a tantalizing look as they walked down the church aisle. By the time she was 15, it was the older men who also were enamoured with her. Her breasts, just through the use of hormones, had grown very shapely, although small, and she enjoyed letting them provocatively bounce up and down as she paraded through the town square braless. She saw no shame in sexuality and fully embraced it, but she had never been penetrated by a man.

She knew that playing with her ass felt erotic, and she longed to be like a regular genetic woman and have a man inside her. She had never tried it, but that was about to change.

Chablis had gotten a job working in the grain mill after school. The owner, Augustine Perez was a handsome man of 33, and Chablis found him very sexy. He was actually almost as short as the now 5:3 Chablis, but he had thick, muscular arms, a well-defined chest and a smooth face, except for a pencil thin mustache that made him look debonair and taciturn. She had seen him staring at her often, but he had been too polite to suggest anything.

Chablis was simply a young woman who knew what she wanted in life, and at this particular time she wanted Augustine to deposit his seed in her virgin ass. That day after school, she hurried home and took a bath rather than her normal shower. She wanted to make sure that which she was going to offer to Augustine was clean and fresh. She even dabbed a bit of perfume on her ass cheeks. She had a devilish smile as she strolled through the village toward the mill. Her friend, Alegra Gonzales saw her smile and immediately ran up to her and said, "You look like the cat that swallowed the canary. What are you up to, girl?"

Chablis, never one to mince words, said, "Alegra, I am tired of hearing you brag about how good Alejandro is in the sack, and how his stiff member tickles your insides. I am about to see how it feels – only from the other end."

Alegra, laughing, said, "So who is the lucky guy about to get the full Chablis treatment?"

Chablis, never breaking stride as she continued towards the mill with Alegra almost running to stay with her, said, "I am going to give Augustine the fuck of his life. It is going to be so good he will probably remember it on his death bed."

Stopping and panting from trying to keep up with Chablis, Alegra stood and shouted as Chablis continued toward the mill, "You go girl."

Ironically, Augustine had spent many a night fantasizing about Chablis. He was unmarried and even thought about leaving the narrow-minded little village and living with Chablis some day in Mexico City when she was 16 and could be free of school. He was too timid and reserved to ever approach her, but his desires often overwhelmed him, sometimes driving him to a sexual frenzy that was nearly impossible to control as he watched her work. Often he would slip off to his office, lock the door and masturbate while peering out the little window that looked out on the factory floor where he could see Chablis moving about, wiggling that gorgeous ass and making her braless breasts bounce about with delight.

Chablis had known for a long time what he was doing, and it gave her a tingle between her legs and made her sphincter muscle contract as she dreamed of what it would be like to glide him deep inside her. She wanted to take him in her mouth first to get him ready, but what she really desired was to feel him pounding away. That would make her genuinely feel like a woman.

That day, Chablis made it a point to have no bra or panties on. Her shirt was tied in knot around her midriff and the top three buttons were purposefully unfastened so that her perky little breasts were almost completely exposed. The tight fitting jeans hugged her curves so tightly that it seemed to Augustine that she was almost inviting sex from anyone in the mill. She was a wanton hussy of desire that day, and all the men were having trouble doing their work, so alluring was she.

Both sides of her curvaceous ass were fully defined by the clothing she wore and Augustine wondered if her cheeks would be easy to part so he could shove his stiff member into her. Everything about Chablis that day spelled sex. Just 15, but nearly 16, and with her dark, long mass of slightly curly hair and big brown eyes, it seemed that a kind of sensual steam was emanating from every part of her.

As the whistle sounded for the end of the work day at 6:00 PM, the workers slowly started filing out of the factory, but the wily vixen, Chablis, was tying off one last sack of grain. She turned her head to the right and there was Augustine standing nearby looking at her. Chablis tilted her head and smiled.

She looked down at his crouch and saw that he had an erection. Yes, he was ready and so was Chablis. She very slowly glided toward him, as their eyes locked in the intensity of the moment. He was breathing heavily, and she just kept smiling that mischievous crooked smile. When she got up to him, she reached down and grabbed his erect member and softly whispered, "I think we need to do something about this problem. Maybe its time we went up to you office and let you do something beside masturbate over my sexy ass."

J. Wayne Frye

Chablis: Avenging Angel for the Forgotten
In the City of Lost Hope

He swept her into his arms, lifting her up and cradling her as he bounded up the 6 steps to his office, kissing her passionately on the way. Chablis was now breathing heavily herself in anticipation of the delight that waited.

When in the office, Augustine placed her on the sofa, turned back to the door and bolted it. Chablis stood up, and embraced him eagerly, their mouths locked in passionate delight as their tongues dashed about like lizards devouring prey.

Augustine was moaning as Chablis pulled her lips from his and began to unbuckle his pants. She dropped to her knees and pulled his pants all the way down. His member was almost ready to break through his briefs when she said, "Step out of your pants."

He immediately stepped out of his tennis shoes without even untying them. His pants fell to the floor and Chablis began to kiss his member through the briefs, reaching around his back and gently pulling them down. It popped out and slapped her on the lips, much to her delight. She cupped his low hanging balls and let her fingers run up his shaft, and his member began to twitch. She knew if she was going to get what she wanted, she would have to be careful, because he was so excited it would not be long before he exploded. She slowly licked the tip of the head, and gently massaged his balls. It was beautiful thought

Chablis, and if she had more time, she would have savoured what she was doing, but she wanted something else.

Just as he started to tense up and explode, she pulled back, stood up and kissed him, her mouth warm from gorging on his member. She whispered, "I have something special for you, Augustine, something that will bring you more pleasure than you ever imagined possible. You want my hole don't you? You want to plunge that monster way up in me and leave your seed inside me don't you?"

She turned and moved deliberately toward the desk, removing her blouse as she did. Stopping at the desk, she pulled her form-fitting jeans off very slowly to maximize the anticipation for Augustine, exposing the most magnificent ass Augustine had ever gazed upon. Her pelvic bones accentuated the deep curve of her small waist, her dark skin contrasting against the white desk. She leaned over, jutting out her ass and reached back to separate her cheeks, moaning for that which she craved. As she heard him approaching, she whispered, "Take it baby, but it needs to be moistened so it will glide in smoothly."

He dropped to his knees and buried his face between the beautiful soft cheeks and moistened it intently, as Chablis removed her hands, letting the crack ease together so it would entrap him; make him work to moisten that which he desired to enter.

Augustine stood up, and despite his intense arousal, he wanted to be gentle with her. But Chablis did not want him gentle. She reached back, grabbed his throbbing member and said, "Give it to me hard Augustine. Give it to me hard."

Chablis' warm ass rolled against his huge member. He reached around and grabbed her breasts. Her tits were even perkier than he had thought and her skin was so soft and smooth! His member shuddered as he began pushing it between her cheeks. He held her tight as his hands roamed all over that soft, hot skin. She was sweating as much as he was and his hands were sliding into the crack of her ass, pushing her soft, downy cheeks further apart, as he felt the hot opening seem to pulsate with excitement. She moaned as she said, "ram it in baby, ram it in."

He licked her neck and face, finally sticking his tongue up into her mouth as she turned to kiss him. His hands started kneading her terrific ass. She was grinding her ass in the air for him, pushing it onto his hot member. He reached down with his two thumbs, trying to pull the opening further apart to make the passage wider. Used to genetic women, he reached around to feel her wetness in her other hole, only to grab that which he had never touched on anyone else but himself. He did not hesitate to play with it, because he kept telling himself, "This is a woman. Yes, this is a woman. This is more woman than I have ever had."

Chablis let out a long, slow, wanton sigh and completely relaxed her muscles. She had never done this before, but she instinctively knew how to take it. Augustine, mesmerized, watched with fascination as his member vanished inside her. She bucked to meet each stroke, letting out a guttural sound each time. She was pushing her ass, grinding it and lifting it higher and higher as she swallowed more and more! The hot friction made Augustine pound harder and harder. It was like his member was being gripped in a hot, fleshy vice, and he loved it!

He pushed once more hard and Chablis yelped. He wasn't hurting her! She was moaning and pushing her ass harder and harder into him as she wanted all of him inside that tight, hot little opening. His pubic hairs were flush against her cheeks and they were both trembling with pleasure.

Chablis was crying: "Give it to me baby! Give it to me hard!" And he did! He gripped her breasts harder with each stroke and let his sweat drip onto her back as he pushed and shoved in and out of that torrid little opening.

Chablis: Avenging Angel for the Forgotten
In the City of Lost Hope

He felt Chablis spasm hard and convulse as he plunged deeper into her. He felt the climactic surge begin and he pushed all the way inside her as he exploded like a cannon burst. He was grunting as his thick hot fluid gushed into her and she seemed to collapse from ecstasy, breathless, exhausted and satisfied.

Her cherub bottom was lovingly shaped,
So round and plump with exquisiteness.
Arched up, she met each thrust with glee,
Her passion like a raging storm at sea.

Between those soft pert cheeks,
Upon her fragile quivering soft skin,
rested his instrument of love,
as she longed for each shove.

The sweet nubile vixen Chablis
Saturated his soul and flooded his being.
She was a wanton, lustful delight,
Making his soul take flight.

Quietly she sighed an erotic tune.
She snaked and gyrated with pleasure.
As deep inside her went each thrust,
there was passion, ardour and lust.

Chablis was a Goddess of light.
She was a beacon of sexual thirst.
His explosion rattled her soul,
Writing satisfaction on passion's scroll.

The two of them became lovers, but Chablis refused his entreaties to move in with him, to in effect be his wife, even though it was not legal for them to marry. She learned that she had incredible power over men, and that she could exert almost complete control with her sexual prowess. Fools, she thought, men are such fools and so easily manipulated.

CHAPTER 2
RESSURECTED WITH A FURY

At an early age, Chablis used to visit her aunt in order to watch television, because her parents could not afford a TV set. Her favourite shows were old detective movies on a station that played 1940's movies. It was at about 9 that she began to ask her aunt why there were never any female private detectives. Her aunt replied, "Because that is not a lady-like profession."

Chablis replied, "Well, it may not be a lady-like profession, but I am going to be one when I grow up."

In adolescence, she was a voracious reader, and particularly enjoyed Dashiell Hammett, Mickey Spillane, Raymond Chandler and Agatha Chrisite. She dreamed of being the female Phillip Marlow or Mike Hammer. At 16, she graduated from high school one year early, and told Augustine she was off to university in Mexico City. When he asked how she was going to pay for it, she replied, "The only way I know how."

Augustine, after a year as her lover, cringed at the thought of her prostituting herself for an education. A soft-hearted man who loved her dearly, he said, "Chablis, I will get you an apartment in Mexico City, and I will pay your tuition. You have brought so much joy to me, and

I am not just talking about sex. You have lifted me up from the despair of a life where I felt trapped, because my family insists that I tie myself to a life in a place I hate. For me, this will be one way I can repay you for your kindness and for lifting my spirits."

Chablis had never told Augustine she loved him, because she did not want to deceive him in any way. She had made it plain to him that their relationship was not a promise of fidelity on her part, because she felt she was too young for that. She smiled, reached over and took his hand, "Augustine, you are a dear man, and any woman would be incredibly lucky to get you. However, I plan to explore my sexuality in Mexico City, and that would be unfair to you. Here, you have given me nothing but your time, and an occasional trinket out of affection. I could not in good conscience take your money."

Augustine, looked into her dark brown eyes and said, "You have never been unfair to me Chablis. You have always been above board in letting me know that you refuse to make me your exclusive lover. I would expect nothing from you, except maybe allowing me to stay with you when I come to Mexico City. I am going to miss you terribly."

Chablis, a grin slowly etching its away across her face, turned around and backed her shapely posterior against his crotch and wiggled it provocatively. She looked back over her shoulder and said, "I know what you are going to miss."

Grabbing her around the waist, Augustine turned her around and kissed her passionately. "You know that I look at you as more than just a piece of ass."

Seeming to melt in his arms, Chablis looked up and said, "Yes, I know Augustine. I wish I could say I loved you, but I have never lied to you and I never will. If you want me with that understanding, OK."

Chablis looked at life as if it were a house. It could be really comfy. However, sometimes it gets cold and you need to turn on the heat. Sometimes, it's too warm and you can't breathe. So you just need to open a window. And that's basically what she was searching for in her life, a bit of fresh air. She cared deeply for Augustine, but she knew he was not her future. That lay somewhere far beyond her village and Mexico City. Augustine was stuck, but she refused to be hemmed in by family, by convention, by religion, by any barrier that was erected to constrain her.

She accepted his offer, and they went to Mexico City, where he got her an apartment near the university. She did not feel like a whore, because she was giving him something he needed, and, in return, he was giving her something she needed.

And besides, both of them did deeply care for one another. It was just that Chablis was not in love, and she never deceived Augustine about her ultimate goal. Everyone in the village knew about the arrangement and Augustine's family was so irate that they threatened to cut him off without a cent. His reply, "do as you will, Chablis is my responsibility and if you cannot live with that, then cast me out, and I will reside with her in Mexico City, where I will get a menial job and be free of all this bigotry that permeates this village like a cancer that cannot be cured."

Augustine's family unwillingly accepted his relationship with someone whom they considered a freak of nature, but many in the village actually respected him for coming out publicly with what had been an open secret for a long time. Augustine's public embracing of Chablis seemed to somewhat break down a wall of prejudice that had been erected against a girl who simply suffered from a birth defect. She had been born with the wrong body, and now it appeared that many people were recognizing that it is not the body that defines gender, but the mind. Meanwhile, Chablis was busy learning English and studying criminology. She had one goal in life. She was going to eventually make it to New York City and be a private detective. She had already been scouring the phone books in hopes of finding an agency to take her on as a trainee. The one at the top of the yellow page listings was

J. Wayne Frye

Aaron Adams. She was going to write him when she was a senior, and ask for an internship, which she hoped would eventually lead to a job, because she had found out that Aaron Adams was the best shamus in New York.

On her holiday visits to her parents, she felt that she had garnered more respect from the people of the village. She had always been smart, but now it appeared that people looked at her differently. The only educated people in the village were Augustine and his brothers, sisters and parents who had all been to university. Now, Chablis was showing that the common people could also get an education. Suddenly, her being a transsexual seemed to be less of an issue with people. Well, most people. There was still Father Hernando, who had always looked longing at her perky breasts, almost licking his lips when he gazed upon them. One day he stopped her in the village square, and hypocritically told her that she should stop trying to be a woman and be what God had intended. She defiantly stuck out her now even more alluring bosoms and said to him with a coy smile on her lips, "God makes mistakes all the time. He put a dick on me when it should have been a pussy. He also made a mistake when he allowed an asshole lecher like you be a priest. He could do with a little more talent when it comes to how he makes people. He should take a course in anatomy and one in psychology. That way he might be better skilled at matching genitals to the mind, and maybe he would also learn that people like you are not suited for the priesthood. You'd be better suited to run a whore house, so you could ogle all the girl's tits and asses like you do mine."

Father Hernando took a deep breath, stepped back from her like she was an evil incarnation, and just as he started too let lose with a vindictive tirade, Chablis cut him off by walking away as she said, "I would say fuck you, but that is what you would probably love for me to do you, old pervert."

Walking boldly down the dirt street, her chest stuck out defiantly, she purposely swivelled her hips a little more than usual to give Father Hernando a good look at what he craved almost as much as her tits. Her gorgeous ass wiggled seductively under her tight-fitting jeans and she had a smirk on her face. It felt good to put the old hypocrite in his place. There was smug satisfaction in doing what she had always wanted to do. She was Chablis Louise Chavez, a woman who yielded no ground to those who wore a mask of piousness to hide their deceitfulness. Damn, she felt good!

While in university, she did not experience as much prejudice as she had back in her village, because she was exposed to people who were not bound by religion and bigotry that was so prevalent in small villages and towns, where ignorance often was encouraged rather than discouraged, because ignorance let the wealthy, the powerful and the church keep people bound in invisible chains of control.

She was actually very popular with the boys at university, but she was careful whom she dated, and she always kept Saturday night and holidays free for Augustine, never wanting to hurt his feelings, because she valued his love so much, despite the fact that she could never utter those words to him. Augustine so longed to hear them, but Chablis had simply chosen a path that would eventually lead her away from Mexico, and she knew Augustine was bound by duty to his family and could not follow her on the path she had chosen. Although unable to marry her at the time, because of laws that prevented such unions, Augustine begged her to live a life of leisure as his domestic partner. However, Chablis tearfully turned him down, because she felt her destiny lay elsewhere.

Her final year in university included a three month internship, and she managed to get Aaron Adams to take her on as a protégé at his New York City detective agency. Aaron found Chablis to be a young woman with immense potential. After graduation, he helped get her a work permit and she went to work for him. She was his number one operative for several years, but right after she became a U.S. citizen, she decided to strike out on her own. She had always dreamed of having a little office like Phillip Marlow in *The Big Sleep* or Mike Hammer in *I, The Jury,* with her named spelled out in script on a glass door.

Aaron, eager to help her, offered all the assistance he could. After helping her get her office set-up, it was then that Chablis finally decided to act on her strong desire to have sex with the man she felt a strong attraction for. While working for him, she knew it was not wise to get romantically involved, but now she had rented her own office and she felt the path was clear to get what she had wanted so long. Still, she was not sure if Aaron would go for her. He was as straight a man as she had ever seen, but he was also open-minded and never questioned her womanhood. She had told him from the very beginning that she was a transsexual, and he had never batted an eye. Would he go for it like Augustine did? After all, she was a pretty alluring woman, and she had even heard Aaron say once, "What is between your legs does not define gender." So, he obviously saw her as all woman.

Chablis had sat many a trap for men over the years in her tiny Manhattan apartment. It had been the scene of some wild fornicating, and now she was determined that she was going to make her greatest conquest. She poured Aaron a drink and walked over to his chair and made sure she leaned over far enough for her braless breasts to flop

J. Wayne Frye

almost out of her low cut blouse. She moved toward the sofa, making sure to accentuate the sway of her hips. Sitting down, she crossed her legs, purposefully letting her rather short skirt hike up until her thighs were thoroughly exposed. This was going to be fun she thought.

The human body is a work of art, and Chablis was a Rembrandt masterpiece. She was feeling like an animal, an animal of lust. And the good thing about animals is that they know no sin, and Chablis looked upon sex as a recreational activity, so she had no inhibitions whatsoever. This was a wonderfully wanton woman.

Aaron nonchalantly seemed to be ignoring her. However, he could not completely ignore her, because he was aroused. He felt a rise in his pants, and tried to get his mind off her by saying, "So Chablis. Why is it so important to strike out on your own? We had a pretty good thing going. What is it that motivates a beautiful young woman like you to want to be in a shady business like this? I have never been able to figure it out."

She leaned slightly forward, her right breast almost falling out of her blouse that she had completely unbuttoned except for the two bottom buttons. "Aaron, I am like you. I love the underdog. The one ignored by society and tossed into the trash bin of despair by those who have no heart and no soul. I just love the people at the bottom of the socio-economic ladder, because they have no one to be their champion. I want to be the shadow that stalks any discontent that might affect their lives! I want to be the scourge of the arrogant, self-indulgent, arrogant and shallow who dismiss them with dispassionate unconcern. When these people suffer, I want to emerge from the shadows to ease their pain. I want to right the wrongs and bring compassion, grasping them with love and respect for that which they really are – noble people trying to survive in a society that aggrandizes greed as an enviable trait. Ah, how I long to embrace these people, and find the peace that floats like a puffy cloud on the distant horizon, so that I can rest confidently knowing I have done all I can for them."

Aaron, fully enjoying looking at her magnificent legs, smiled and said, "You have listened to my rhetoric too long, Chablis. You have become too passionate about the order of things in a world where the few rule supreme."

Chablis leaned back on the sofa and replied, "You have been a good teacher Aaron. Most of all you have taught me the joy of fighting for the underdog, the satisfaction that comes from knowing you have taken a stand against injustice and the pride that comes from making sure that those who are fodder in the vile machinery of capitalism that grinds people up are able to stand up to their oppressors by hiring us to ferret out the evil ones who get rich on the backs of the exploited. You have helped give me a sense of self-worth. I can do things I never dreamed possible. I am going to be the second best private eye in New York."

Then she got up abruptly and almost raced to embrace Aaron, who had a quizzical look on his face as she bent down and kissed him passionately. Their tongues went exploring. Chablis was sighing as she pulled her lips from his and whispered, "I have wanted to do this ever since I was your intern Aaron. I have dreamed of the moment when you would plunge deep into me and deposit your seed, but first, I am going to give you the greatest blow job you ever had."

Aaron eased back in the chair, closed his eyes and just sit still, breathing shallowly as Chablis crawled between his legs and began to unzip his pants. She slowly removed his shoes, and then Aaron raised his hips so she could slide off his pants. She pulled them off furiously, tossed them on the floor and began to gently tug at the elastic band on his briefs, as Aaron again raised his hips so she could get them off easily. She looked at his member as it flew to attention. It was not as big as Augustine's she thought, but it was cut, and she bent down and kissed the tip lightly. Then she began to talk to it. Yes, she was actually carrying on a conversation with it. "Each night you gorgeous thing, I dream about you. I dream about licking you, tasting you, swallowing you. Each night my dreams of you are laden with fire, as I am overwhelmed with desire for you. I am tossed about by a savage, raging desire to possess you. I want to thrust you into every part of my body and devour you." Then she gorged herself on it, as if she were a starving woman who had just come upon a feast. Aaron thrust upward, meeting each downward push furiously, slamming against the back of her throat as she moaned with pleasure and he let out guttural sounds. Suddenly, he felt it rising up from the depths. Yes, it was on its way up the shaft to make its way out the tiny opening with a fury so hard that it slammed into the back of Chablis mouth, and she gobbled it up like it was the essence of life, sighing loudly as she felt a sense of exhilaration that she had brought Aaron such pleasure and satisfied her own desires in the process.

Sapped of energy, they both lay there for a few seconds, she with her head buried in his crouch, nuzzling his thick member and blowing on it and Aaron just breathing slowly, totally exhausted from the experience. He had never had sex with a transsexual before, but he had no qualms about it at all, because to him, she was 100% woman.

Chablis, who never knew any shame in her life, looked up at Aaron and smiled. "If it is the dirty element that gives pleasure to the act of lust, then the dirtier it is, the more pleasurable it is bound to be. When you are ready dear Aaron, I am prepared to give you the ultimate pleasure. I want your seed one more place."

Aaron had been through the back door of lust many times in his life, but this was to be his first time doing it with a transsexual. He reached down and pulled Chablis up into his arms and kissed her. As he was embracing her, she began to unbutton her blouse and her perky breasts flopped out against his chest. She reached down as they were kissing and started removing her skirt, pushing it down, down, down until she wiggled out of it and it fell to the floor. She still had on her panties, and Aaron began to wonder how she kept it hidden so well. He could not feel her erection. Had she lost the ability, he thought?

Just then, Chablis rose, pivoted 180 degrees, turning her back to Aaron. She started moving toward the sofa, making sure that she accentuated every sway of her ass. She slowly peeled off her minuscule panties, stepping out of them as she glided gracefully forward. Those beautiful, perfectly formed cheeks gyrated provocatively as she moved over to the sofa arm, being careful that Aaron could not see her now stiff member for fear that it might turn him off, and not allow her to get what she craved so much. Lying over the arm of the sofa, she reached over to the coffee table and picked up the KY jelly that she always had handy just for moments like this. Meanwhile, Aaron moved deliberately toward the sofa, never taking his eyes off her magnificent ass that was now profusely jutting into the air. She squeezed some KY out, reached back behind and placed it delicately into the little brown pucker hole and waited – waited for the coming ecstasy that would soon be overwhelming her.

Aaron moved behind her, placing his member in the crack and began to rub. She reached back and glided it to where she wanted it. She moaned and prepared for the thrust of pleasure that would soon overwhelm her.

She was not disappointed. Aaron was slow and methodical, being careful not to hurt her. He saw Chablis as a delicate creature. Yet, his steady, deliberate thrusting was perfect as she relaxed and waited for Aaron to get all the way in. They both let out a sigh of satisfaction as he felt himself smoothly reach the limits of penetration and he then began a steady, rhythmic pounding, his loins making a slapping sound with each thrust forward against her cheeks. Aaron looked up at the ceiling for a second, and felt as if he was in another dimension, so intense was the pleasure. It was then that Chablis started thrusting back against him, meeting each forward projection. They were in perfect sync now, moving toward a climax of monstrous proportions. Like crashing thunder, Aaron exploded a torrent of joy juice deep inside her and they both moaned with delight.

There is lust and there is love. They can often be one and the same, but Aaron and Chablis knew that they were not in love. This was just one lustful interlude that would never be repeated again. They were dear friends and would remain so the rest of their lives, but the sex was a one-time thing that seemed a necessity to get the sexual tension between them abated once and for all. Aaron said to Chablis as he was leaving, "You are a gem that sparkles with radiance. You are polished steel that is smooth as silk. I am always here for you Chablis. Anytime of the day or night, I will be there for you. You are a most remarkable woman, not because of your sexual prowess and openness about fornication, but because you are a woman with a heart and soul that cries out for compassion."

Chablis, at 5:3, a great deal shorter than Aaron, raised herself on her toes and kissed him on the cheek. Rocking back on her heels, she looked up at him and said, "You will always be the rock upon which I rest my weary soul."

Aaron smiled and said, "When I first met you, you were a caterpillar, but you have become a butterfly." He turned and walked away. There was an intense simpatico between them.

The whole course of life can depend on a change of heart in one solitary and humble individual, because it is in the solitary mind and soul of the individual that the battle between good and evil is waged and ultimately won or lost. However, we all are capable of both good and evil. We must strive to make sure the good rises to the surface while we suppress the evil. It is a constant struggle for many people, and for some, the good is sublimated for only a very brief time, but that time can alter so many lives. What has been discussed previously prepares the reader for what follows, because it is a story of how in a single split second when evil is allowed to rise to the surface lives can be altered. As a raconteur, I have laid the groundwork for a story that now will unfold in detail, as the reader observes the emergence of Chablis Louise Chavez as a force to be reckoned with by those who dare stand against justice. So now, we began to explore that which makes this a tale of an unintentional inextricable web of deceit that would lead two people in search of the truth – the truth that would bring a dark shadow into the bright light. To say it is a tale of woe would be true, but it is also a tale of hope. It is a journey into a nightmare of anguish, but it is also a trip into the corridors of endurance in the face of adversity.

Chablis Louise Chavez was about to find love and acceptance, but in the process she would face betrayal of the foulest kind from the man she loved. She was a free spirit, but not so free that she did not have deep rooted insecurities when it came to keeping a man she genuinely loved.

Chablis: Avenging Angel for the Forgotten
In the City of Lost Hope

She met Andy Deluca in a small out-of-the-way coffee shop, and sat there for 4 hours drinking coffee and talking. They met again that evening for dinner and a movie, and Chablis was hesitant to tell him something that was never obvious, because she was more woman than most genetic women. Still, she knew that it must be done as quickly as possible to avoid recriminations. She found herself asking if he would be appalled when she revealed that she was a transsexual. She had lost a few men that way, but it never bothered her, because she always figured if it bothered them they were not worth having anyway. She was a woman and never doubted it, and, to their credit, most men did not let it prevent them from enjoying the company of an extraordinary woman. When it got down to sex, most men she dated were straight, so they avoided what was between her legs. That was alright with her, because her eroticism was not there anyway. It was in her shapely, alluringly magnificent ass.

So, as she sat on the sofa with Andy, she scorned his incessant attempts at kissing her, because as she always said, "I never want anything to happen under false pretences. The best way to get yourself beat-up is to let a homophobe find out what you are all about after he has kissed you, fondled your breasts or allowed you the pleasure of placing your mouth around the root of his passion."

As she pushed Andy away one last time, she said, "Cool down Andy. I want you very much, and I certainly know you desire me, but there is something I must tell you."

Andy sat up and got a deadly serious look on his face. "You aren't going to tell me you are a man are you? Damn, if you are, I might go gay!"

"No, I am not a man. Do you know what a transsexual is? I am a transsexual."

Andy sat up straight and almost glared at her. Chablis just knew she had lost him, but he said as a grin slowly etched its way across his face, "Of course I do, and I know you are a woman. Chablis, I am already in love with you. I was the minute I set eyes on you. I knew you were a remarkable woman." As he concluded, he leaned forward and reached out to pull her to him, and this time she melted in his arms willingly, their mouths finding one another and passion overtaking them.

Chablis was smitten with his working class charm. He was uncouth, even downright rude with his garish behaviour at times, but she, for some reason, found it endearing. His belching in public, passing gas in front of her and his habit of leaving the bathroom door open when he performed the most basic of human functions were just overlooked by her as the actions of a man was not privy to the normal social graces of polite society. Rather than being offended, she somehow accepted it as part of his good-old boy charm.

However, she did not realize there was a sinister element beneath this persona of "ah shucks" innocence. Aaron, upon first meeting him, could see the façade he was using to captivate Chablis. He tried to talk to her about the shallowness of the man, but she was in love, and Aaron eventually gave up. He was there at their wedding four months later. He felt emptiness inside, because he had deep feelings of friendship toward Chablis. She was like a daughter to him, and he desperately wanted to protect her. Yet, love erects a barrier to the truth, and Chablis simply would not entertain any thoughts of this man being less than her knight in shining armour.

When Andy asked her to give up her career and let him support her on his window washer's salary, she willing left her trendy apartment in Manhattan and moved over near the Bowery, where Andy had a one bedroom walk-up with only one window. She was giving up everything for Andy, and did it willingly to show him how much she loved him. After three years of marriage, she turned her back on Aaron, who kept pleading with her to not walk away from her career as a private investigator. Aaron was preparing to leave for Stockholm where he would become involved in the famous case chronicled in the book *The Girl Who Stirred Up The Whirlwind*. His final plea to her to exercise more caution in dealing with Andy, was met with her usual disregard at the airport as she said, "Aaron, I love you dearly, but for three years you have tried to get me to turn my back on the man I love. Go to Stockholm and find this girl Jasmine Alexander and save her from certain death. I do not need to know anything more than I already know about Andy. He is my life now, and nothing is going to change that."

Aaron, his head bowed, walked toward the gate. He turned and looked back at Chablis, sighed deeply and said, "Subtlety may deceive you; integrity never will. One woman rarely suffices for most men, so they deceive by telling you that their heart is only reserved for you. They do not tell you that what is between their legs is spread around freely." Aaron moved toward the screening machine and never looked back to see the quizzical look on Chablis' face. He intended to plant a seed of doubt within her, but Chablis refused to doubt her beloved Andy.

Chablis thought about what Aaron had said, analyzed it, and then dismissed with little thought the idea that Andy would cheat on her. Absurd she

J. Wayne Frye

thought. She whispered to herself under her breath, "Hell, I am a beautiful, alluring woman who keeps him sexually satiated from my conjugal demands, how cruel of Aaron."

She walked away, feeling hurt that Aaron would even suggest such a thing. She reflected on Andy's insistence that she meet him at work every day so they could ride home on the subway together. Now that was real love, as was the little smiling faces she got on her cell phone throughout the day from Andy. She was too naïve to realize meeting him every day at work was more ego gratification than love. Andy enjoyed watching his fellow workers look at Chablis. It made him feel important to show-off his possession. And the constant texting was not love; it was a method of control to make sure she was not out with another man. He had to keep tabs on his property. Even the marriage licence, to Andy, was like a dead to his property.

As she caught the IRT for downtown, she did have one thought that planted a small seed of doubt about Andy's sincerity. She had wanted his entire family to know she was transsexual to avoid the possibility that they would find out and be shocked, but Andy had said, "That's between you and me. Nobody else needs to know." Was that, she thought, a sign that he was ashamed of her?

No, that couldn't be it. No, that was impossible. Yet, this was the very first time that she had a small tinge of objectivity when it came to Andy. The time would come when she would be even more objective, but for now, she was too much in love to let that absurdity play upon her mind.

Still, as she sat on the subway she began to reflect on what she had once read. There was a duality that is in all men. There is a child in all men – a child that needs constant reassurance of manhood. Wisdom can only be acquired. One is not born with it. That is why the older man is more grounded, more able to think before acting, because emotion in the young overrules logic. Andy was young, so did that mean he was capable of infidelity? No, no, never.

Andy always called Chablis, "my little honey bunch." That was his pet name for her. It was a special thing, from him to her he always said. He would bring his face down close to her ear and whisper it low. He would say she was his honey bunch, because she was so sweet. Then one day Chablis noticed it had just stopped. She waited patiently for it to be whispered, but it wasn't. It had disappeared from his vernacular.

One day he stopped asking her to come to work to meet him, and then he started going out to meet the boys for drinks, poker or bowling. Strange she thought but no reason for alarm. Hey, the honeymoon was over. Life settled into a routine. He was just looking for a little escape from the domesticity of married life, not to worry.

One day Chablis was rummaging through the closet for a dress when she noticed that Andy's one suit was missing. She kept looking around the large walk-in closet, wondering what could have happened to it. She noticed his favourite grey shirt was missing, too, and she had just washed and ironed it a few days before. She asked him about it when he came home, and he said, "Oh, I took both of them to work with me. I had an important meeting and wanted to shower at work, get cleaned up and look my best."

A lie now and then where there was no reason for a lie is not the norm thought Chablis. She reflected on the evening he had spent with the fellows. No harm in that, but it had become more frequent lately.

Yeah, that last night with the guys, he had said they all played poker at Harley's place in lower Manhattan. No big deal with that, but then when Harley showed up looking for Andy one day and when she mentioned the poker game, Harley had a quizzical look on his face and gave a cagey, noncommittal affirmation of Andy's presence. Out of the corner of her eye, she had noticed Andy give him a glare and a wink.

Then there was the powder compact that she found in his jacket pocket. He saw her looking at it and he told her how he had happened to find it. People do lose compacts. Even nice silver ones engraved "To Mai-Mai from AR." Then, on the very next day after that, no compact was there when she checked the pocket again. She asked him what had become of it. "Oh, I got rid of it," he said in a shaky voice as he lowered his head to avoid contact with Chablis' eyes.

"You got rid of a silver compact? I could have used it."

"No honey, I don't want you to use somebody else's compact. It's not sanitary."

How stupid does he think I am thought Chablis. After all, I may have quit my job to satisfy him, but I was a private eye. Come on – get real. Then, she had an uneasy feeling that happiness was beginning to slip away. Little things like missing clothes and a strange compact were beginning to establish a pattern.

Still, Andy had never given her any reason to question his fidelity. After all, he was insanely jealous of her, even threatening to kill any man who dared try and as much as flirt with her. Why he had even once confronted a colleague at work, demanding that he not talk to Chablis while she was waiting for him outside the building where he was cleaning windows. And what about the cell phone he insisted she carry at all times so he always knew where she was? Why would he be so jealous if he had something on the side? Yeah thought Chablis, she was flattered by the jealousy and the control he tried to assert. He was just insecure and felt he had to keep close tabs on Chablis. Hey, it was understandable; she could do a lot better as Andy really had nothing going for him. So, he was naturally guarded having such a beautiful woman in his bed. Yeah, nothing to worry about thought Chablis. Needless to even consider that Andy could cheat on her, it couldn't happen.

Chablis remembered what she once read in a book, "I know I am but summer to your heart and not the full four seasons of the year." Yeah, was she no longer the four seasons to Andy? Had she lost her ability to keep his interest in only her? Doubt was now forming in Chablis' mind. Had Aaron been right all along? Had he seen something in Andy that she simply could not fathom?

There is a moment, sometimes only a fraction of a second, when love seems to trickle from the spout of hope and fall into the puddle of doubt. It can be a tiny phrase that he no longer utters, a glint in his eye, stumbling for an explanation to the inexplicable, always going out with the boys when he used to relish her company, going to bed and not reaching over to caress her or say "I love you" and the ignoring of the niceties which were once the norm.

Suddenly the name popped into Chablis head. What a strange name, Mai-Mai. Then she remembered. Yes, she remembered. She went into the kitchen recycle can and started throwing newspapers all about. There is was, yes on the back page of the entertainment section was an ad for an off-Broadway play and who was staring in it? Mai-Mai McCloud, who else?

Instincts die hard, and Chablis had been the second best private eye in New York City, so her instincts were not dead. They were just dormant. However, they were about to be resurrected with a fury.

CHAPTER 3
MAKE A HOUND DOG TALK

Chablis' detecting instincts kicked in as she began to almost delight in getting to the bottom of what was becoming a perplexing mystery to her. The business of the suit was one thing, then there was the compact. Circumstantial evidence was beginning to pile up. She walked over to the hallway closet where Andy kept a medium size suitcase. She crouched down beside it, and the latch tongues wouldn't open; they were locked. Why? He had never locked the suitcase in three years of marriage. Why now?

She picked it up and it was so heavy she had to strain to hold it. What was in it? What was Andy up to? Had he put some clothes in it? It was big enough for a suit, some shirts and toiletries. She called his cell phone, but for the first time in three years, he did not answer. She caught hell if she did not answer his texts or calls, but he was different all of a sudden.

Chablis just stood there for a minute holding the cell phone, staring at it, fondling it as if it was a connection to Andy. Yes, it was a connection to Andy. It had been his method of control for three years now. Then in a flurry of action she headed to the bedroom and opened the bureau drawer. She took out her 38. Why she asked? Why was she going to start packing again? What was she expecting when she confronted Andy? Would he get violent? He had been on the verge of it a few times, but always backed down. Once, he had even raised his hand in preparation to deliver a blow, but she had stood her ground staring him down. Yet, she was not going to take any chances. A confrontation was coming.

Then she moved casually back toward the hallway closet, pulled the folding doors open and just stood there surveying it. What was she looking for? Scanning up, down, side-to-side, her instincts were getting fine tuned again. Then she noticed the carpet was not completely tucked against the wall in the right hand corner. It had obviously been pulled up and then pushed back down.

Chablis dropped to her knees and crawled to the corner. She gently pulled back the carpet, being careful not to touch the tacks holding it down. There was a manila file folder underneath. She carefully removed it, open it up and there was an 8 by 10 photo of an incredibly beautiful woman, the same woman in the newspaper. It was Mai-Mai. The newspaper photo did not do her justice. She was a brunette like Chablis. Her eyes were wide and languorous, and her lips thick and sensual. She had an air of aloofness about her. There seemed to be an almost evil arrogance about her. She was beautiful, knew it and wanted the whole world worshipping at her feet.

That was all there was in the folder, just the picture. Chablis, looking at it with great consternation and trepidation could not figure out why Mai-Mai would want anything to do with her man. After all, Andy was not handsome in the true sense of the word. In fact, he was rough looking and his pock-marked face usually had a scowl on it. He was overweight, was missing two teeth on the left side that showed a gap when he smiled. Chablis had fallen for him because of his shy charm and because he wanted to marry her. He had been the first man since Augustine to be that committed. She had even been told by friends like Aaron that she was just settling for him, because he wanted to marry her, and all the other men just wanted erotic satisfaction from a woman they looked at as an anomaly.

Chablis did not bother to put the folder back under the carpet. She just tossed it on the shelf in the closet. She then thought for a few seconds just staring at it, reached up and took it again. She would not put it back. She wanted to hang onto it. She whispered to herself "I am also going to hang onto Andy, bitch."

Chablis leaned back against the hallway wall, staring at Mai-Mai's picture and hating her hard. A fury was building within. Chablis was now growing angry, but as always, she controlled it. She was focusing and was in deep thought about what to do.

Chablis: Avenging Angel for the Forgotten
In the City of Lost Hope

She went into the bedroom and started getting dressed. She took more pains getting dressed, making herself look wickedly seductive. Well, she was always seductive looking, but this time she was accentuating it to the extreme. Chablis had the kind of seductiveness that let everyone know she was in touch with her sexual energy and so in sync with her freedom of sexual thought that there was no act between consenting adults that was not permissible. She was a sexual animal and walked around like a magnet, attracting men who were desperate for her attention. She knew she was alluring, but was not arrogant about it. Her seductiveness came from her ability and tendency to focus on the personal and emotional state of others. She always set an alluring tone by quiet confidence demonstrating that she liked herself, that she enjoyed the person she was with and that she appreciated the experience the person was offering. In an instance, she could brighten the outlook of the man or even the woman she was seducing and heighten their responsiveness, ultimately lifting the quality of the experience at hand. An evening with Chablis was to be savoured and reflected upon for many days, months or years.

For Chablis in her prime, when she was free of the restraints placed upon her by Andy, her seductiveness was all part of living life in the most fully human manner possible. She made life feel like one great big playing field where effervescing

J. Wayne Frye

seductiveness comes out to play and eroticizes everything else that stands in the way. She inspired all who observed her "let's live life with intensity" attitude. Nothing she said or did was rehearsed or scripted. Everything happened spontaneously, unfolding at that very moment, right then, right there. She was adaptive, ever-changing and always ready for adventure. This lent a mysterious quality to her persona that captivated men and women alike. Ah, how envied she was for doing things her own way with no restraints. Well, none until she met Andy, anyway. But now, motivated by that old urge to "strut her stuff" she was TNT ready to explode. She once again was resurrecting that old primal sexual power that would lay low all rivals before her. This was Chablis Louise Chavez, ready to rock and roll!

It was not men she was dressing for but for Mai-Mai. Chablis could stand-up against any woman when it came to being a seductress. Mai-Mai was the enemy, and Chablis was about to go into battle.

Finally she was ready and got out fast. She left so quickly, closing the door with a loud slam behind her, that she forget her cell-phone that Andy used as a method of keeping tabs on her to make certain she was not seeing other men. Yeah, thought Chablis, for three years he has been keeping a weary eye on me, when it is I who should have been keeping an eye on him. Damn, Andy was such a hypocrite!

The city of New York is a microcosm of America. There was great affluence as displayed by the ostentatious few, but most people were either in abject poverty or struggling to keep their heads above water. Ironically, through well-coordinated propaganda, the few kept the many wrapped up in the belief that the opportunity for the good life was always out there if you were just willing to work hard. As Chablis walked past the countless, mindless, country-loving, God-fearing, flag-waving, manipulated slaves to the bottom-line of corporate America, she realized that what the city needed was an avenging angel to wreck havoc on those who preyed upon the weak. Aaron Adams was just such an angel, and Chablis had been one, too. Yet, she chucked it all for the love of a man who had mesmerized and manipulated her for three years now. Well, she was about to sweep down on the city again and all who stood against justice and fairness had better step aside, because this avenging angel was a force to be reckoned with.

Mai-Mai's place was one of those remodelled former mansions that had been converted into apartments, but of the expensive, not the cheap, variety. It was the type of place that offers extreme privacy, including a doorman to keep out the riff-raff. Chablis whispered to herself, this doorman will be a pushover for a hot body and a pretty face. Then again, aren't most men? Men were so dumb and easy to manipulate and the doorman was also young, probably hung and extremely dumb. It would be a piece of cake.

She was going to enjoy this. She had been imprisoned by Andy's jealousy for far too long, and now she was blasting her way out of the cocoon of control. Sauntering up to the doorman with her perky little breasts exposing maximum cleavage, she purposefully jiggled them by accentuating her stride to make them move up and down rapidly. The young man was nearly creaming in his pants as his jaw dropped and his breathing quickened. What fools thought Chablis, what goddamn fools.

Moving slightly toward her, he stuttered a greeting. "Ah, ah, hello ma'am, May I assist you?"

Chablis, for maximum effect, looking down at his crotch, replied, "Sure, I am certain you can be helpful to all the ladies."

Taken aback by her boldness, the young doorman's pupils began to dilate with excitement as he muttered, "Wha-wha-what ma'am?"

"I said I am certain you are helpful to all the ladies. A good looking young man like you must get lots of offers for the delights of the flesh."

The doorman could not believe Chablis' boldness. His stuttering responses continued. "Why-why, I-I don't know what to say."

Smiling that crooked smile that started on the right side of her mouth and crept slowly and methodically toward the left side, Chablis said, "Just say yes big boy. I am really horny."

Seemingly in pain from the erection that was pressing against his pants, the doorman was more flustered than ever. Chablis bent over. Letting her tits press against his chest, she said, "Go in that broom closet over there and pull your pants down. I will walk in, drop to my knees and give you a blow job that will make you think you are having sex with a vacuum cleaner."

The doorman did not say a word. All he did was take a deep breath, turn and scamper to the broom closet, gently closing the door behind him, leaving it slightly ajar.

Chablis smiled and thought "you still got it girl," as she glanced over at the tenant directory and immediately found Mai-Mai McCloud. Bounding up the stairs to room 208, she giggled a little thinking about the doorman waiting patiently for the blow job that was not coming. Hell, he would look at the elevator to see what floor it was going to, but Chablis had used the stairs. He would be too embarrassed to report the incident. He would just ignore it and hope for the best. She went into the small forward vestibule that jutted out from all the apartments and found Mai-Mai's name above a doorbell, but before she could put her finger to it a man bearing a small package came strolling out nonchalantly, nearly bumping into her. He politely held the door for Chablis, but never really raised his head, keeping it tucked low and covered by a wide-brimmed hat. He scurried away, so she stepped in unannounced. That way, she avoided being refused admittance by Mai-Mai.

Suddenly, a wave of concerns ascended upon her. What the hell was she doing? Was all this necessary? Why not just confront Andy?

She saw the whole episodic journey there as preposterous, unlikely to succeed in accomplishing anything. Then she quickly looked over by the sofa and saw two suitcases by its side. The bitch was going somewhere.

As Chablis stood there, she thought to herself, "why am I here? I am acting like Andy, being controlling and checking up on him. Hell, which is what he did, because he was so possessive and scared that some other man might attract me."

Chablis' mind was racing now. "What do I expect to get out of this? What possible good will it do? If Andy is gone, the son-of-bitch is just gone. Who wants him anyway, now?"

Then she looked closer at the bags. Damn, one of them was Andy's suitcase. She was leaving with Andy, but for where?

The hopelessness of the thing she was about to do began to overwhelm her. What was she doing in this woman's apartment? Hey, she was Chablis Louise Chavez who had never bowed before adversity – that is what she was doing there.

She cleared her throat and said, "Ms. McCloud!" No one answered, so she spoke a little louder, "Ms. McCloud!" This time she heard a faint echo as there was a reverberation that almost made Chablis fearful. Her instincts told her that there was something terribly wrong.

Chablis looked around and took in the ambiance of the room. It was a great pleasure to the eye, but there was something barren about it, as if there was no heart or soul that went into the decorations. There was a distinct immorality about the place, a complete lack of character. The apartment was simply too perfect. Nothing was out of place, absolutely nothing. It did not look lived in. Chablis turned to her right and saw her reflection in the giant wall mirror that was there, no doubt, so Mai-Mai could bask in the glory of her own reflection. The whole place bespoke of a vain woman who was probably as meticulous in her appearance as she was in the aseptic approach to her decorative manifestations.

Something seemed to draw Chablis to the bedroom. She very slowly moved forward toward the slightly ajar bedroom door. The ornate door had gold hinges that sparkled in the sunlight that was peeping through the slight opening in the curtains. Through the door opening she could see a small area of the bedroom that was done in bright red. She saw that even the duvet was red. Chablis thought to herself, "A real den of inequity where my husband, no doubt, enjoyed carnal delights with her."

As she was almost to the door, she peeped at the clothes that had been randomly scattered all across the room. No doubt, the woman was in a hurry to get out of the place, as her meticulousness had been tossed aside for expediency. She must have dressed in a hurry thought Chablis. She shifted back and forth just standing there, wondering what she should do.

No one was there. It was obvious. Chablis turned around and wandered back to the living room and sat down on the sofa beside Andy's bag. She just lingered there, staring off into space. She slowly scanned the surroundings and she noticed everything was monogrammed. Even the custom made sofa had the initials *MMM* on the cushions. The curtains had it. The recliner had it. Then, as she looked down at a half empty wine glass, there they were, her initials were on the glass. How vain thought Chablis.

Suddenly the telephone began to ring. She sit perfectly still for a few moments, waiting for it to quit. It didn't. It kept on and on. Where was the damn answering machine thought Chablis as she stared at the phone sitting on a small desk near the window? Finally growing weary of the noise, she got up and walked over to the desk. Standing there looking at it, as if a stare would stop the ringing, she noticed right beside the phone was a little address book, with its thick leather cover stamped with the same inevitable monogram. Chablis lifted the receiver finally to try to silence it. Then, for some reason, she put it to her ear, stood quietly and listened. A man's voice said instantly, and with a sort of hurried intimacy, "Mai-Mai?" That voice. Chablis would have known his voice anywhere. She put her free hand down on the desk to steady herself. The room began to spin and a kaleidoscope of memories cascaded through Chablis' mind. Yes, it was Andy on the other end of the phone. She could not find words. Standing there, staring at the monogrammed curtains, teardrops formed in her eyes as she very gently placed the receiver back in its cradle.

Chablis walked haphazardly back toward the bedroom door, stopping at a table where Mai-Mai's picture sat in a heavy silver frame. She seemed to be mocking Chablis with a look of arrogant disdain. The kind of look she had often endured in her little village from people who saw her as a freak. Memories long forgotten boiled to the surface. "Damn that woman," she said out loud.

Hate was never a part of Chablis' character, but at that moment she felt intense, unmitigated hatred of the foulest kind for Mai-Mai. She could not help it. She thought about smashing the picture, but what would that accomplish? Sighing, she moved back toward the sofa, seemingly unconcerned about being in a woman's apartment uninvited. There was a chaise lounge chair near the bedroom door pulled out about three feet from the wall with that customary *MMM* embroidered on it. She noticed a bedroom slipper lying on the floor in front of it. Yeah, she thought, I wonder where the *MMM* is on it. She moved over to pick it up and noticed a foot projecting out from behind the chair.

A hideous clarity of what had happened immediately crystallized as she moved behind the chair and looked down at an obviously dead Mai-Mai. There was a pillow lying beside her head, obviously used to smother a scream and, probably, to snuff out her life. Chablis had seen death before, so it was not shocking in and off itself. What was shocking was that she had wandered around the apartment, even been seen by a man leaving. Could he have been the killer, or like her, just wandered in and found the place empty and left without seeing the corpse. Chablis had been so concerned with confronting Mai-Mai that she had not really been that observant of the guy. She could not even recall his facial features.

Still looking down at the body, the death grimace was etched on Mai-Mai's face, her tongue was hanging out the side of her mouth and there were indentations on the carpet where she had apparently dug in her heels fighting desperately for a breath that never came.

Staring at the corpse, Chablis scanned the room for any clue that might be apparent. Everything seemed exceptionally tidy except for the bedroom slipper that was on the floor. Well, and of course, the body. Then she honed in on the leather-bound address book by the phone. Yeah, in that book might be the killer's name, but it might also contain Andy's name and that would connect him to the murder. Chablis had to prevent that. She had been betrayed by Andy, but he was still her husband, and she knew he was not capable of murder. Anyway, why would he call if he knew she was dead? Of course, she had dealt with the cops before. They were not always the ripest apples on the tree and would often hone in on a suspect and nonchalantly send the wrong man up the river just to clear a case load, especially if the guy was poor and/or uneducated. Andy was both.

They mustn't connect him with her thought Chablis. They mustn't know he'd known her. Yes, that address book had to be removed if Andy's phone number was in there. She went running over, picked it up and leafed through it. There it was, not inside the book but right on the cover. His cell number was actually underlined. First she was just going to tear the cover off and leave the rest behind. Then she realized that would be too obvious. Determined to protect the man who had betrayed her, she stuck it in her purse.

She started toward the door, and then remembered the suitcase. That would be traceable. She picked it up and on the way out the door she noticed a small part of a matchbook cover lying on the floor with the boldly written letter **R** on it. It had been torn in half, and that was the reason the door had been open. Someone had wedged the matchbook cover in the hole of the latch. It could have been the murderer. She walked out of the apartment with the piece of the cover and headed down the stairs. Dumb she thought. Yeah, I am really a dumb jilted broad who got in the place, but how am I going to get out? She would not have to worry about the doorman, as he would be too embarrassed to admit he had been in the broom closet with his pants unzipped waiting for a blow job, but he had no idea Chablis had gone upstairs, so how could she get out without being noticed?

She stood in the stairwell at the top of the stairs with the suitcase by her side as she was in deep thought about how to get out of the building unnoticed. What would my mentor Aaron Adams do she asked herself?

She could hear the doorman moving about but could not see him. She looked at the broom closet. It was right near the base of the stairs. How could she get him to go into it? If she could get him in there for just a second, she could leap down the stairs and slam the door on him and hurriedly run out, go into the nearby alley and get away with him only seeing her from the back. Yet, he would remember her as the woman who had lured him into the broom closet, because he would recognize her clothes even from behind and her cascading beautiful black hair would no doubt clinch the recognition quotient.

Chablis knew that virtue was not going to get her out of the spot she was in. When virtue is lost benevolence appears, when benevolence is lost right conduct appears, when right conduct is lost, expedience appears. Expediency is a shadow of what is right and can be very disorderly. However, Chablis had to initiate disorder to make certain she was able to get out and not be discovered. Disorder and confusion were her only hope. She eyed the fire alarm on the wall, walked over and used her elbow to smash the glass. The fire alarm went off immediately, and she heard the doorman run toward the elevator to hit the lock key so no tenants could use it during what might be a serious fire. As he stepped into the elevator doorway, she quickly moved into the lobby, elevating the suitcase with both hands and slammed it so hard into the doorman's back that he tumbled forward with a thud. She kicked his feet into the elevator and the doors closed before he realized what happened. Chablis bolted out the door and was in the alleyway in a flash. Never looking back, she strolled out of the far end of the alley slowly and blended in with all the people walking down 43rd Street as if she were just a lady heading out of town with her suitcase in tow. She hailed cab and headed back home. Andy was going to really catch some hell when he got home.

Chablis thought to herself on the way home that Mai-Mai's death would let her keep Andy. Damn, she hated herself for loving him so much. Why she asked, why was so infatuated with an uncouth, ill-mannered, illiterate, overweight slob like Andy. Was it what he had between his legs, and he sure had plenty? Was she that shallow?

When she got home, she simply walked to the hall closet, hung up her coat and placed the suitcase behind the clothes hamper and shut the door. She needed time, a little time to pull herself together. She kept saying, "I am Chablis Louise Chavez Deluca, a woman with an iron constitution, a woman with real balls!" She laughed as she thought that statement was literally true. When she said she had balls, she really did and she had just proved it. Damn, the adrenalin was pumping away. She was actually enjoying herself. She suddenly realized she missed all the action, all the excitement, all the risks of being a private eye. However, this was no cat and mouse game conducted for a paying client. This was about a murder that her husband could be implicated in. She rushed into the bedroom and began to get a bit frumpy, smearing off her bright red lipstick, removing the sexy garments for jeans and a T-shirt and kicked the high heels under the bed and put on flip-flops. That was the way Andy preferred her. Hell, he had even encouraged her to eat more. Maybe, thought Chablis, he wanted her fat. That way, no other man would be interested and his property would be protected. Damn, that was the way he looked at her. She was his property. Their marriage licence was not a certificate verifying their marriage. It was a deed signifying that Andy owned her. That was the way Andy looked at it. He owned Chablis, but apparently he wanted to expand his investment portfolio by including Mai-Mai. Well, that investment had just gone sour.

Chablis was cool under fire. She had just proved that. She actually was feeling exhilarated, but there was more trouble coming. Andy would be home soon.

She began to feel better, grew calmer and decided to brew herself a cup of black coffee. Suddenly she shook her head in disgust with her amateurishness. Andy already had a suitcase there. Damn, how stupid I am she thought. He would be going there after work. He was planning on leaving Chablis for the dead bitch. If he went over to Mai-Mai's, he might be there when the police arrived and become the number one suspect.

She had always looked upon the cell phone given to her by Andy after only two days together as a method of control that she just accepted as a price for marriage. However, now she was glad she had it because she could warn him to stay away from Mai-Mai's. He was treading on thin ice anyway, as he had tried contacting Mai-Mai while Chablis was there. He might have repeated that again, since she left and even left a message. Damn, that would lead the police right to him. Chablis thought to herself that she was out of practice being an investigator and was getting careless. Still she had taken the precaution of removing the address book with his name in it, yet it had never occurred to her to take the greatest precaution of all by forewarning him.

She dialled quickly, lamenting that she had waited so long. The voice mail popped on after five rings. Damn, he must have the phone turned off. She could not leave a message warning him, because the police might confiscate his cell phone. All she did was just say "Come home right away Andy. Don't go anywhere else, please." She was breathing heavily now, trying to contemplate her next move to protect Andy from the coming calamity.

It was 2:50 PM and Andy got off work at 3. He was working only ten minutes from home. Yeah, she could make it. She could catch him as he came out the door. As she bounded down the stairs two steps at a time, she recalled that German movie *Run Lola Run* where a girl was desperately running toward a planned robbery to save her boyfriend from certain death. Yeah, she could make it just like Lola did. She flew out the door like a madwoman, nearly knocking down a man who was entering the building. She had no time for apologies. She just kept running.

Rounding a corner at the end of the block, Chablis began to wonder whether she was running to something or running from something, or maybe both. She had to save Andy, even if he had betrayed her, so she must run to him. He could display machismo when he was casually talking about killing anyone who dared look at Chablis in a lustful way or dispatching those who questioned the culture of greed that he had been propagandized into believing was the best economic system in the world. He had even said all communists should be lined up and shot. Yeah, he was an anachronism, a throwback to the 1950's who believed a woman's place was in the home, but actually murdering someone – no way he could do that – no way.

Chablis: Avenging Angel for the Forgotten
In the City of Lost Hope

She bounded down the street, her braless breasts bouncing wildly up, down and sideways, and her perky nipples were straining against the tight T-shirt. Even though her breasts were about 40% plastic, they had begun to sag a bit in recent years, so she looked as natural as any other woman her age.

Of course, there was nothing natural about a woman running frantically down the busy streets of Manhattan. People were staring intently, some even asking, "What's wrong," but she had no time to answer. Andy's future was in her hands. She was racing against time.

Chablis was almost defying the laws of physics as she bounded through the streets, seemingly with both feet off the ground at times, literally flying above the sidewalk. Was she willing herself into an alternate reality? The pace and power within her were exploding in a cacophony of guttural sounds emanating from her. Her heart was racing so fast that it seemed to be beating a cadence like a kettle drum pounding out a fanfare. Two blocks away she thought – two blocks from saving Andy. As she stopped, waiting for the "GO" signal in the crosswalk, she bent over, trying to catch her breath, sucking in as much air as she could. Looking at the red light saying "Stop," she was wondering if Andy was worth it. Hell, he was seeing another woman. Why was she trying to save the son-of-bitch? Was it love or was it the knowledge that jails were full of innocent people in a country where justice was only reserved for the well-off?

"Go" flashed on and she began her furious run again. She glanced across the street at the clock above Bank of America – 2:57. Andy always left late, because he wanted his colleagues to see his beautiful wife meeting him. It gave him great ego gratification. Yeah, thought Chablis, I'll give him some gratification right between the legs where it hurts the most. He might prefer the police to me she thought.

Chablis, her head raised toward the blue sky, recalled an old tune:

You need somebody who likes them-self
Who lives for life and never calls for help
You need somebody to walk you back
Someone who loves you too before you ask
You're worth more, you're worth more than this
You can take a leap without the risk
There's no time, there's no time for this
Take your love and start again
So run for your life
Run for your life
If you leave me behind
You'll get there in time
You need someone who can stand alone
Who finds the way, instead of being shown
Somebody with confidence

　　　　　J. Wayne Frye

Chablis: Avenging Angel for the Forgotten
In the City of Lost Hope

Who's strong enough to be hit more than once
You'll find more, you'll find more than this
Take the world that's at your fingertips
Don't waste time, don't waste time on this
Take your love and start again
So run for your life
Run for your life
If you leave me behind
You'll get there in time
Run, run and don't look back again
Run, run, one day you'll understand
I'm not, no, I'm not who you think I am
So run for your life
Run for your life
If you leave me behind
You'll get there in time
Run for your life
Run for your life
If you leave me behind
You'll get there in time

Yeah, why was she running for this man? Why didn't she just leave him behind like the lyrics said? She had thrown everything away for him, and he had given her nothing but a few expensive gifts that he couldn't afford. He thought love was bought, not earned. Suddenly, Chablis was reflecting on the ridiculous nature of the relationship. Still, she was his wife, and the marriage vows meant something to her, even if they didn't mean anything to him. She was not going to abandon him until she learned the truth.

Chablis: Avenging Angel for the Forgotten
In the City of Lost Hope

He was capable of a lot of things, including violence as more than once he was on the verge of physically assaulting her, but backed off at the last minute. But murder, no way was he capable of that. Anyway, the phone call proved he was not the killer. Why would he be calling for a woman he had just killed? Well, the cops, with their convoluted way of thinking would say he was just establishing an alibi. Andy was poor, and in America, the poor were always suspected. The police were nothing but storm troopers dedicated to protecting the wealthy and powerful.

One block left. She could see the building now. Damn, she had made it. She almost stumbled when a guy jumped out of a cab at the curb and bumped into her. He tumbled to the pavement, but she had no time to stop and assist him up. She just kept ploughing ahead, never wavering in her determination.

Running down the street of hope,
Chablis was now shedding tears,
Thinking she had made it there in time.
There was the building of steel
And relief was all she could feel.

Breathing heavily she recalled,
The love she and Andy had shared.
It had soared high and free
Like a butterfly spreading its wings,
But reality often stings.

Chablis: Avenging Angel for the Forgotten
In the City of Lost Hope

As she peered at the glass tower,
She saw a reflection in the door.
A cab was pulling away from the curb.
There was Andy in the back seat.
Chablis suddenly felt defeat.

Turning rapidly she called out,
But he never turned his head.
Exhausted from her run,
She rested her back against the glass,
Realizing the die had been cast.

There was no chance she could reach him in time now. He was going to Mai-Mai's place.. The slender thread of hope had snapped. Chablis felt no remorse about not reporting it to the police, because that would have only solidified the predicament. Hey, she thought, even the police would not think a killer would be stupid enough to return to the scene of his crime. The police could be stupid at times, especially when dealing with the poor, and Andy would certainly qualify as poor since $50,000 a year was only a marginal income in New York City. So he would probably just be questioned and then released. Sure, they might hold him, but his innocence would eventually be evident.

It was getting late, and the sun disappeared behind some clouds. Chablis thought that the light of hope had been dimmed, too. She had always recognized Andy as a somewhat shallow man with no real hopes for the future. Even his job washing windows was a give-me, as his uncle had gotten him the position, because he felt sorry for him. Before that, he had been delivering pizzas.

Chablis had questioned why she stayed with him for three years, as she watched Andy live a lavish lifestyle he could not afford. Why had she tied herself to the man? Why did she give up everything for a man who lived on the brink of insolvency all the time? Why did she submit to his constant control and manipulations? Was it because she was flattered that a person from a class of people who were rough, uncouth and bigoted accepted her when others didn't? Still, he had shown that he was actually ashamed of her by saying. "You being transgendered is between you and me. No need to tell my mom, dad, brothers, sisters or colleagues." Yeah, Chablis thought, the son-of-a-bitch was ashamed of me, and here I am trying to save his ass. The world had changed a lot over the years, but people like Chablis were still on the outside looking in. Deep down she was still that little girl who longed for acceptance from a society that only toyed with the idea, but in the end it just wasn't there. After all, she was fighting for justice in the land of hypocrisy. She remembered a sign she once read over a door into a social services centre.

> Those who enter here are accepted and embraced. Character is the centrepiece of a person's true worth.

Chablis: Avenging Angel for the Forgotten
In the City of Lost Hope

Chablis exhausted from the difficult run, strolled back home and waited and waited and waited. She wondered if he even had any intention of coming home to say, "I am leaving you." She even asked herself why she cared. He was a cheating son-of-a-bitch. Yeah, why care?

It was long past time for his arrival from work, so he had gone to the apartment and was probably being detained thought Chablis. He had missed that inane show about swamp people that was passed off as history on just another network that had ditched decent programming to cater to the lowest common denominator. Every day she had to endure that ridiculousness while she fixed dinner, and he sat in the living room laughing at asininities. Yeah, well at least with him gone she wouldn't have to watch all the stupidity that passed as entertainment.

She kept glancing at the clock, wondering if she should go to Mai-Mai's apartment. No, no, that would just be counter-productive. She just stood staring at the clock on the wall. The little jumping noise it made as the hand ticked off the seconds made her feel like screaming. It was incessant – click, click, click, click.

Why was she so worried about a man who was cheating on her? She hated herself for worrying about him. She raised her hands to her brow, rubbed it and sighed. She began to pace up and down the hall, always looking back at that damn clicking clock. Click-click-click, the sound began to reverberate through her head – click, click, click, click. At one point she was considering yanking it off the wall and throwing it out into the outside hallway to be free of that infernal clicking noise.

Then finally, Chablis simply had enough, she couldn't stay away from that damn apartment any longer. She had to know what was going on. She grabbed her coat, kicked off her house shoes and put on a pair of canvass loafers. She was nervous, but still able to maintain her decorum. She wrenched open the door, and like a soldier ready for combat, she swept into the hall, slamming the door behind her. Shoulders reared back, lips pursed together, tightly gripping her handbag, staring straight ahead with determination she had that old swagger back. Damn, she almost felt good, because, like days of old, she was once again ready to go into battle against overwhelming odds. This was the old Chablis Louise Chavez. She didn't even stop at the elevator; she walked down the stairs, almost bounding down them as if gleefully anticipating the coming battle. She thought to herself, "Should I go back and get the 38? Do I want to really go into battle without a weapon? Hell yes, I don't need a weapon, I am Chablis Louis Chavez, and I am packing the deadly weapons of determination, drive and desire. Look out world, here I come."

Chablis: Avenging Angel for the Forgotten
In the City of Lost Hope

As she exited the building, she came to an abrupt halt as there was Andy, getting out of a police cruiser. He had a forlorn look on his swollen face as two burly men in those dark suits always worn by police detectives, one on each side of him, held his arms tightly and ushered him forward. Chablis moved toward Andy and reached out to touch him. The detective on the left gave her a stern look and motioned with his head for her to back-off. It was uncanny; it was almost like a resurrection of sorts. Chablis actually felt exhilaration over what was going on. She was back in the fray. She was alive again. For so long she had lived a cloistered existence as Andy wanted to protect his property from exposure to anyone he felt was a threat to his control, because if he lost control, she might see the shallowness of her existence with him.

He'd been in a fight. As if Chablis gave a damn. Hell, she would have given him that cut lip, that lacerated eyebrow, that bloodied nose if she could have gotten hold of him. Well, maybe she did give a damn – just a little bit, because if it was the detectives who had done that to him, then it was a matter of that "good old" police brutality that was used against the poor. Arrest a CEO on Wall Street and the detectives would be stopping to get him a latte on the way to the police station. The standards of justice in America were just like the economic system; all the good things flowed to those at the top.

Chablis kept waiting for someone to say something.. Andy looked too scared to utter a word. Finally, the detective on the left said, "You Chablis?"

Chablis, never one to cower before authority, replied, "No, I am Mrs. Deluca, sometimes known to you flatfoots as Chablis Louis Chavez, private investigator. I know you Carlton," she said to the detective on the right, "I once testified against you in court in regards to a beating you gave to my client, who was an innocent man." Then, looking at Andy who had been obviously beaten, she continued, "and I see you are still carrying out your usual methods of interrogation."

Carlton's back stiffened and a look of intense recognition overcame him. "Damn, Chavez. You are a chick with a dick. I remember you."

Chablis, now seeming to enjoy the verbal sparring, said, "I am a chick, period, asshole!"

Carlton said, "You may be a chick, but you are no damn lady."

Smiling, Chablis replied, "I am always a lady Carlton when I am around gentlemen, but that isn't the case right now."

The other detective, taken aback by the verbal war between the two, interrupted. "Hey, let's go upstairs, we need to check out the apartment. You two can continue your war of words at another time."

Chablis said, "Carlton, I have a question for you. You got a warrant?"

Carlton very sternly said, "We have probable cause, Chablis. You know the law. Don't need a warrant. That is the trouble with you shit-house lawyers; you learn all your law on television or on the streets. You going to lounge out here on the streets where you belong Chavez, or you want to escort us up?"

Andy tried to say something but only got out an "ah" before Carlton pointed his finger and said, "Shut it Deluca, you will talk when we are ready for you to talk."

Chablis said, "Carlton, I will escort you up, but as for belonging on the streets – a prostitute has more integrity than you do. They are rendering a valuable service that brings happiness to many people who are lonely. You are an overpaid masochist who should be in prison right along beside all those people you beat confessions out of."

Andy still hadn't said a word. Chablis winked at him, turned and walked back into the building, the three of them following her. Ah, what a pleasure it was to follow Chablis all three must have thought. As the old song goes, "The way she wiggled when she walked would make a hound dog talk."

CHAPTER 4
CHABLIS LOUISE CHAVEZ
IS BACK IN BUSINESS

Chablis couldn't take her eyes off the handcuffs that had Andy's hands locked behind his back as she stoically stood in the hallway while the three of them walked in front of her through the doorway into the apartment. Typical she thought that even before the accused is brought to trial the punishment already starts. The uncomfortable way of binding people's wrists behind their backs was a form of sadistic torture enjoyed by the so-called polite society in America. Meanwhile, the rich, when arrested, were just told to turn themselves in at the police station with their high-priced attorneys in tow.

Finally, Andy spoke-up, "It's OK Chablis. I am innocent. They can't convict me of a crime I didn't commit."

Chablis, shaking her head in total disgust as she nonchalantly watched the two detectives carefully scan the living room like soldiers reconnoitring for an assault, replied, "Andy, they can convict innocent people and they do all the time. The jails are full of innocent poor people who couldn't afford a good lawyer, or people who were frightened into confessing to a crime they did not commit. There is no justice in this country except for the rich."

Carlton, who had stepped a little further into the living room, turned with a sour look on his face and said to Chablis, "Bitch, if you don't like the way things are run in this country, pack your bags, grab a tortilla snack and hit the road back to Mexico."

Chablis smiled and replied, "I wouldn't give you the satisfaction. I am going to stick around to watch you finally get what you deserve, and I may be the one who delivers the coup-de-grâce. Of course, being an ignorant low-life like you are, I doubt if you even know what coup-de-grâce means. I'll define it for you – it is the final blow, the death blow delivered mercifully to end suffering, but I might let your agony continue for awhile just to get one last laugh before you are dispatched off to hell where you belong."

Carlton, a grimace on his face turned to the other detective and said, "Keep an eye on him Johnson and also on that bitch. I'll toss the place."

Andy looked scared. He said to Chablis, "I didn't kill Mai-Mai. I didn't Chablis. I-I-I" he stuttered almost incoherently, "you-you know there was a ...."

Chablis, wanting to make sure that he not utter anything that could be used against him put her index finger to her mouth to indicate he should shut-up.

Johnson, seemingly a bit more professional than abrasive Armand Carlton, said, "Listen to the lady, fella. Best to keep quiet until you talk to an attorney."

Carlton spent a lot of time in the bedroom and then walked back into the hallway and into the walk-in closet there. He was rummaging around, and Chablis worried that he might find the picture. No need to worry as he was very thorough. He found it and then walked out with the suitcase in his hand also.

Smiling, Carlton, looking at Chablis, and then at Andy, said, "So, you have a picture of the deceased woman and a bag all packed. Going to skip town I suppose."

Chablis said, "You moron, he couldn't have killed her. Don't you see, he was washing windows down at the Riley Building? Why would he be stupid enough to kill a woman, and then go back to the scene of the crime? "

She was talking to ice. There was no feeling there. Even his eyes were ice. They were fixed on Chablis, and the daggers were piercing her heart so intense were they. In her years dealing with Carlton, she had never been able to figure out whether he hated her just like he would any other person or did he have a special hatred for transgendered people?

Carlton placed the suitcase on the floor. "So, your man couldn't have done it? I am a moron? We'll see who the moron is. This suitcase is packed, because he probably called you and told you he had killed a broad, so you packed it for him. Maybe Chablis you are an accessory after the fact."

Chablis just stood there with a smirk on her face. Carlton knew she was not afraid of him, and she also knew that he had no proof, no reasonable cause to arrest her. With Andy, well, he was on pretty solid ground. The DA would probably toss the charges, because they wouldn't stick, but they could make Andy's life miserable for awhile, and Carlton enjoyed that very much. He loved making people squirm.

Carlton let out a crooked grin. "Chablis, it's wonderful how you go to bat for your guy."

Chablis, tired from the verbal war simply said, "Carlton, he was washing windows all day at the Riley Building. Check it out."

Almost laughing, Carlton said, "We did that. Seems he was on a lunch break from 11:00 AM until Noon. Seems he took it at a different time than usual today. No one saw him during that one hour. Guess what bitch, the broad was killed between 11 and 12. Seems like your boy here is made to order for this killing. Just a few formalities and this case is wrapped up." He looked at Johnson and motioned for the door. "Let's go Butch."

Chablis said, "So, she was killed between 11 and 12? Suppose I tell you I was over there around 11:00 and bumped into some guy who was coming out the door with a package in his hand.

Johnson got a quizzical look and said, "You telling us you were actually in the apartment or just outside?"

Disgusted, Carlton said, "Sure, sure. You were there. I am sure a jury would buy the testimony of a guy's wife who says 'please, please Mr. Judge my husband is innocent cause I am his alibi.' Oh yeah Johnson, we should take the cuffs off him. This here broad is his alibi; she knew they were running away tonight, so she just went over to Mai-Mai's apartment where they had tea and Chablis here could bid her farewell and ask her to take good care of her husband."

Chablis knew how sarcastic Carlton could be, but she noticed that Johnson was thinking about what Carlton said. He felt sorry for Chablis, but he was also convinced of Andy's guilt. He said, "I'm sorry Mrs. Deluca that wouldn't help much even if it were true. You see, Andy here can not account for his whereabouts between 11 and 12. I sympathize with your concern for your husband.

My suggestion Ms. Deluca is to get him a lawyer right away. Based upon my appraisal of the evidence against him, he is going to need a good one."

"Quit giving her advice Johnson, this thing here that calls herself a woman was a thorn in the side of the department for years when she and Aaron Adams were both determined that we were more crooked than the crooks," Carlton said with an air of contempt.

Chablis gave Carlton a look of quiet determination and spoke in a measured way without raising her voice. "Carlton, you do the very same thing you arrest other people for doing. You have a badge, and like all people in authority, you think that gives you privilege. It gives you nothing but contempt from people like me who see through your facade of respectability. There are a few people in the department who are not like that, but not many. Johnson here may be one, but if he hangs around with you for very long he will wind up just as corrupt and brutal as you are. Mark this down in that piece of shit thing you call a brain. The day will come when I bring you down. You can count on that, guaranteed. I should have done it years ago, but as of today, I am making it one of the priorities in my life after proving my husband innocent of the crime you want to railroad him for. You and I are going to tangle, and it's not going to be pleasant."

Carlton stared at her and said, "You'll have a damn hard time proving your lover boy's innocence. Andy may have you fooled, but we can put him at the scene. You see, he can be placed at Ms. McCloud's apartment around 11:00 AM, and she was killed between 11 and 12. Your boy here matches up perfectly for the crime. The doorman saw him leaving the building at 11:15, so there is no need for him to even admit or deny it. Your boy here is good for murder 1."

Andy blurted out, "Damn it. I didn't go in. I couldn't get her to answer the bell. So, I waited awhile and then just left."

As Andy finished, he was turned to his side by Johnson who pointed down at his left hand that was cuffed behind his back so Chablis could get a good look at all the scratches and welts. He said, "These were probably from a struggle."

"Her damn cat did that," Andy screamed, continuing to address the two detectives as if Chablis was not even there. "I've told you where those came from over and over. She wouldn't let him in, but her cat was in the hallway and I tried to grab it, and it slashed at me and ran away. It acted like something had frightened it, so I let it go."

"Good alibi, that cat," Carlton said, "but not good enough. Come on. It is time to book you."

Then Johnson gave Andy's wrist a directional jerk toward the door and said. "Let's go."

OK, maybe Andy was guilty thought Chablis, but images of the way America treated prisoners in Afghanistan, Iraq and Guantanamo Bay flashed through her mind. Cruelty was the norm in a country where everything was seen in black and white with no shades of grey. Once again, Chablis thought about how they cuffed people with their arms in the rear, not because of safety, but because it inflicted pain and made the person feel helpless. There was a sadistic nature to so many authority figures in a country that thought it had a right to use terror to fight terror. It was supposed to be a country of laws, but the truth was that the poor and downtrodden were guilty before proven innocent not innocent until proven guilty. That was the American way.

There was something that made men like Carlton love to inflict pain. It made them feel more like men. It was easy to get people to commit atrocities. The wars of conquest in the Middle East under the supreme disregarder of human rights, George Bush, had proven that and the torture chambers at Guantanamo and the drones whizzing over sovereign nations to kill people were a testament to the fact that even reformers like Barrack Obama were willing to ignore the most basic of human rights. So, Carlton was just a lowly imitator of those at the top. He

was just another poster child for cruelty in a nation
that turned its back on atrocities it committed in
foreign nations and on its own shores.

Without any more words they took Andy and
left, slamming the door behind them. Chablis, not
one to cry, wiped a tear from her eye and said out
loud to herself, "The bastard was cheating on me,
but I will still stand by him, because I don't think
he did it, and with Carlton on the case, he will be
railroaded. He may not deserve it, but I'll prove
his innocence. Then, I'll divorce the son-of-bitch."

If you are rich, you can put off a trial for
months, even years, but Andy and Chablis were
poor, so he went to trial in only 3 months, and
Chablis had no time to thoroughly investigate the
case and the little she was able to investigate all
came up negative. She had found out some things
about Mai-Mai, but nothing to connect her to
anything nefarious. One important thing did come
out in the trial. Apparently, Mai-Mai had been
wearing a pin on her blouse and it had been taken
off, because the blouse had pierce marks in it.
Chablis wondered what the significance of the pin
was.

Chablis had told her story to the jury about being
in the apartment, even about running into a man as
she went in, but she was Andy's wife, so it had no
real effect. And then there was the lawyer, John
Folton. Even the name spoke of incompetence as

it reminded Chablis of a former Bush Administration official who was noted for his desire to use force rather than diplomacy. Well lawyer Folton had tried that tactic in the courtroom, bullying and condemning rather than negotiating and persuading. It was all over but the sentencing.

Folton kept telling the obviously worried Chablis that an appeal was already in the works in case of the worst possible outcome. The biggest problem was that Chablis' testimony had no corroboration. So, she said she had vamped the doorman. Well, the doorman said it never happened. Who would they believe, a woman trying to help her husband or a doorman who had no vested interest one way or the other? Nobody else saw Chablis come or go there that day. That was the unfortunate part of it. Corroboration was unavailable as a result. The mysterious man carrying a package out of the apartment was not verifiable either, so the whole case was just open and shut – done, finished, wrapped up with no lose ends.

Then there was Chablis herself. OK, the jury was not informed she was a transsexual, as the judge had ruled before the trial that was irrelevant and could not be brought up by the prosecution. To top it off, Chablis was too appealing, too attractive and too sexy-looking. So was Mai-Mai; consequently, it was obvious to the jury that Andy was attracted to "hot looking" women. Then there was the fact that Chablis was an injured party herself who had been defiled by her husband's abysmal cheating with another woman. The circumstantial evidence was overwhelming and the verdict was never really in doubt.

As they walked to the courthouse, Folton took her arm and said, "Be prepared. I see no chance of him being acquitted, but we can appeal on several grounds. Believe me, all is not lost."

The verdict, as expected, was guilty in the first degree. Fortunately, New York was one of the 18 states that did not have the death penalty, but when the judge sentenced Andy a few weeks later, he did add the caveat – life without parole. So, as always in America, there had to be revenge as part of any sentence. Even the parading of the victims family members up in the courtroom to rant, rave and point the finger of condemnation at the guilty party was part of the revenge process. Of course, Mai-Mai had so defiled her own family, only three of them showed up.

Chablis endured it all with nobility and never displayed any emotion in the courtroom. However, she was more determined than ever to get to the truth. Andy had always denied being in the apartment, even after he was placed there by witnesses. Was there somebody who looked like Andy there, or was Andy lying for some reason?

Chablis: Avenging Angel for the Forgotten
In the City of Lost Hope

Damn, thought Chablis, she needed her old mentor Aaron Adams on the case, but he was in Stockholm, working on what would become the famous case that would be called *The Girl Who Stirred up the Whirlwind*. Still after she talked to Andy, she was going to call him. He had called her in the beginning and said he would rush home if necessary, but Chablis had simply said she could handle everything, but now she needed Aaron's help. He did not have to come home, but she needed his guidance.

That night she called Aaron and was surprised when a young sounding woman answered the phone. Aaron was 62, and she knew that he was in Stockholm looking for a 26 year old woman. Damn, she thought. Aaron was some "old man." He still had that old knack of attracting women with his suave, debonair devil may care savoir-faire. He was old, had a little bit of pot belly and some wrinkles and sags, but he was still the kind of man whom women found attractive, because of his intensity of purpose, his gentlemanly manner, his way of always putting a woman on a pedestal, and, above all, the respect that he showed women. Yeah, she had only had one sexual encounter with him, but it was one she would always treasure.

Giving Aaron the details on the case, he said that he would love to come home, but that his new friend, Jasmine Alexander, was marked for death by an assassin known as the Whirlwind, and he could not leave her in a lurch, because he was all she had between her and certain death. The authorities were going to do nothing, and the C.I.A. was involved now. All hell was about to break loose, because he was onto something really big that would blow the lid off the assassination of Olaf Palme, the socialist Prime Minister of Sweden, back in 1986. For the readers interested, that case is also covered in the same book, *The Girl Who Stirred up the Whirlwind.*

Reviewing the case with Chablis, Aaron asked, "So, is there any indication that something might have been taken from the apartment besides that package that the guy was carrying who went by you?"

"No, nothing Aaron, nothing. Wait a minute. Wait a damn minute, there was obviously a pin removed from her blouse. Maybe he could have had it"

Aaron, a light turning on in his head, interjected, "That is the key, Chablis. That is what will unravel the whole case. That pin is in someone's possession, and that someone is either the killer or is someone who has the key that will unlock the door to the answers you are looking for. You have to find that pin."

Chablis, feeling more confident said, "So, where do I start Aaron?"

Aaron, sounding a bit perturbed that she didn't know where to start, said, "Come-on Chablis, you are a detective. You start with the murder victim. Go back into her past, dig up all you can on her. Most of all, find out who might have given her that pin that was stolen. Whoever gave her that pin might not be the murderer, but there was a reason the pin was taken. Nothing else was taken, right?"

"Right, Aaron. Well, except for whatever was in that package the guy was carrying. It was pretty small, about the size of a cigar box. I can't believe I didn't get a better look at him. His head was down and turned to the right away from me. He was very dapper, a bit thin and had coal black hair."

Aaron was starting to get wrapped up in the case now. "OK, so the guy probably knew her. She was an off-Broadway actress. Check out all the people in the plays she has done, the prop departments, the directors, the producers. Hell, maybe even the people who bought tickets. This is not going to be easy, but you can do it."

"Of course I can. You were right Aaron. He turned out to be a no-good, rotten, two-timing, cheating blue collar Casanova who couldn't keep his zipper up, but I am still not going to let him do time for a crime he didn't commit. Especially since our old friend Carlton is the one who handled the case."

Aaron, sensing that old camaraderie between them said, "Of course you aren't, because you are my protégé, and my protégé would never let injustice prevail without a fight."

Chablis said, "I am on it Aaron. I am also going to bring down our old buddy, Armand Carlton in the process. Chablis Louise Chavez is back in business."

CHAPTER 5
HELL TO PAY

Then one who was wrapped in infatuation and lust
Stood in awe looking up at what he had lost.
He could not see he was better
for being free of her.
She was sitting on the throne of wickedness,
Sipping the dark wine
of vain, destructive malevolence.
She was drunk with her
own beastly, depraved villainy.
She was a woman arrayed in purple and scarlet,
And adorned with jewels
and pearls of maliciousness.
She held the cup of abominations and impurities.
She was the epitome of malignant, malicious evil.

BACK TO THE BEGINNING

In Mai-Mai's apartment building, the doorman was momentarily detained by a delivery at the rear of the building, so he did not see the lone figure, with his head lowered to avoid anyone seeing his face, enter and take the elevator up to Apartment 208. The lone man across the street staring forlornly at the building had also been momentarily distracted by a fracas between two men at the end of the block, so he also missed seeing the solitary figure clandestinely enter the building. It was perhaps propitious irony that he did not see the man.

J. Wayne Frye

Chablis: Avenging Angel for the Forgotten
In the City of Lost Hope

Sam McCloud, shivering from the evening chill and shaking from heartache, stood in the street across from Mai-Mai's luxury apartment on Park Avenue. It was one of the few smaller buildings left. Only 8 stories, it had not fallen victim to the wrecking ball of greed that tore the beauty from the heart of the city as a result of corporate gluttony that devoured everything in its path and left a wave of conformity in its wake.

Sam McCloud was an accomplished piano player who had played in piano bars all over New York City. At 28, he had steady employment doing what he loved, and he was married to a beautiful woman. Then, his life came crashing down around him. His wife, Mai-Mai, left him to run off with another man, then another, then another and another. She simply had decided that Sam would never provide her with the luxury she craved. That was three years ago, and Sam had been on a downward spiral since then, playing for pocket change so he could procure enough to buy his next drink. He had fallen into deep despair, tumbled into a pit of hopelessness as he pined for a woman who had discarded his love, disposed of it without a thought for Sam's pain.

He hopelessly stared up at Mai-Mai's window. It was their anniversary. No, no, it was his anniversary. She had long ago cast him aside for the arms of others who had more immediate potential. He longed to just gaze upon her again, to bask in the radiant beauty of the woman who had become his whole life. Without her, he was an empty shell of a man. He was simply a dead man walking.

As he leaned against the shop window that from behind the safety grating was displaying expensive silver candelabras, wine cisterns, monogrammed serving trays and other items reserved for those who were at the top of the social strata, he reflected on the silver medallion he had bought Mai-Mai on her birthday. It was more than he could afford, but he scrapped together $9200 to get the sea shell cameo that was placed on pure sterling silver. It had been hand-made in Torre del Greco, near Naples, in Italy. It was created by hand by a skilled artisan who carved individual pieces of double layered sea shells with a steel burin. The artisan attached the selected piece to the end of a dub stick using special glue. He then carved from the softer outer layer the incision of a face based on a picture of Mai-Mai that Sam had provided. The likeness was so much like Mai-Mai that it seemed to come to life when you looked at it.

Mai-Mai loved it. It was a treasured adornment that she wore proudly. Yet, only four weeks after receiving it, she announced she was leaving Sam, as she had a man who was going to star her in an off-Broadway production. After all, Sam was just a wandering minstrel, not a real bread-winner, someone who could shower her with luxury the way men who were worthy of basking in her glorious beauty could.

So now here was Sam, where he had been for three years hoping, longing, dying for that which was now gone. He simply could not let Mai-Mai go. She was no good and he knew it. But, without her, he could not exist.

Looking up at the window of her living room, he was trying to muster the courage to go up and hand her the small package in his now profusely sweating hand. It was not a present like the cameo. That was far out of his meagre reach now, but he had played in a few dives around town for tips and managed to save enough money to buy her a silver chain that she could attach to the cameo's ringlet. Oh, if she would just smile at him one more time rather than discard him with her aloofness and cold-hearted disregard. Maybe then he could crawl into a hole somewhere and die, finally find peace. Yes, without Mai-Mai he wanted to die. He had been trying to kill himself with drink, but somehow his heart still beat. Why? Why could he not get the courage to extinguish the breath of life that he wanted to end in the sweet repose of blackness? Without Mai-Mai, each breath was laboured. The sun never came up to brighten the day, because the light that shined in his life had been snuffed out by the wind of betrayal. Forlornly, he wrote a song in his mind:

Chablis: Avenging Angel for the Forgotten
In the City of Lost Hope

You were a star that shined brightly
in the dark skies that surrounded me.
That star seeped through my veins
and became a part of me.
And then I had to put it back into the sky.
That was the most painful thing
I have had to do in my life.
However, even though it's up in the sky
and shining on someone else now,
I still feel its warmth coursing through my body.

As I walk about in a daze,
I have sweet recollections of the woman
who left a map in my mind,
because everywhere I am,
every time I am alone or in a crowd
I have thoughts of you and through silent tears
I recall the deep, abiding memories of the days
when I went on wonderful journeys with you
and felt a part of your life
and sensed that you cared about me
almost as much as I cared about you.

My gratefulness for the time
you shared with me transcends
all else in my life of quiet desperation.
The great love you faked for me
is now reserved for another.
I am sustained by memories of what once was.
I owe you a debt I can never repay.
My heart is bankrupt with pain,
but the mere sight of you

J. Wayne Frye

Chablis: Avenging Angel for the Forgotten
In the City of Lost Hope

brings back the breath of life
that now is smothered in misery without you.

Meanwhile, in Mai-Mai's opulently appointed apartment furnished, not by her riches, but by the riches of the men she used, the magnificence of what she thought was the good life was nothing more than shallowness of a soul that knew no restraint when it came to manipulation and the avarice pursuit of satisfaction that simply was forever elusive. The opulence of the life she lived represented illumination she thought, but it was actually a darkness that could not be reached by any light. Her possessions were all poor and worthless compared to the common light which the sun sends to the windows of the majority who toil in obscurity. That light pours over valley, hill and mountaintop kindling the sky of hope with reason, conscience and love. It offers a dignity of worth rather than the indignity of avaricious greed found in the lives of people like Mai-Mai.

Mai-Mai was at her dressing table combing her lustrous blond tresses when her maid came in and asked if there was anything she wanted form the market, as she was off to do the shopping.

Not a woman of politeness, Mai-Mai replied, "If I wanted anything I would have left a note on your to-do board in the kitchen like I always do. You have been here long enough to know that. Leave me alone."

Used to the abuse, the Hispanic maid lowered her head, turned and as she was leaving said, "Yes mum." Like so many of those who come to America in search of a better life, she found work serving those who looked with contempt upon the people who are the life-blood of a nation that shows no respect for the poor who must toil in obscurity to survive. As she left the apartment, she closed the entry door, but did not hear the lock catch. She thought to herself, "Fuck it. Who cares?" She walked through the vestibule entryway which had no door, only an unlocked gate for architectural charm and refinement that was expected in a Park Avenue apartment. As she made her way to the elevator, she did not notice the solitary lone figure hungering in the stairwell watching her leave. On the witness stand, she would insist that the door was locked, so Andy's key provided another link to the murder of Mai-Mai, despite the fact that Andy had actually packed it in the suitcase that Chablis had brought from the apartment. It made no difference whether it was in the suitcase or not, Carlton had decided Andy did it, so he never bothered to look for another perpetrator, and with an attorney like Bolton, conviction was a foregone conclusion.

Ah, but let us not wilfully digress to that which had already occurred. Let us continue in our exploratory journey into that which was unfolding before Andy was convicted, because what happened that day as Sam McCloud stood outside pinning for Mai-Mai was going to play a significant role in Chablis' pursuit of the real culprit. A pursuit that would connect her up with Sam McCloud and lead her to love, genuine love for a man who would make Andy seem like a long lost memory of stolid infatuation.

When Sam had Mai-Mai, he felt like he owned the world. He was free of despair and soared above the mountains of hopelessness. Now he was empty inside. There was a hollowness that made him nothing but an empty shell of a man.

It is the invisible that Sam was worshipping – the invisibility of a woman who simply did not exist. He exalted that which was illusionary. He saw something that was not there. It was a hallucinatory delusional fantasy of a woman who was more a myth of his mind than reality.

Sam did not realize that the music of love must be played by two. It is not a solo performance. You must push all the right buttons to bring life to love. When a heart breaks, that is when you find whether there is real love or not. Is there compassion or indifference? When the cold storm of the world blows winds of discontent that is when you must find that sunlight together that will shine with the soft reflection of the divine radiance of love. Mai-Mai was only capable of a solo performance, and Sam simply did not realize that. He genuinely believed that Mai-Mai still loved him – just a little. Yeah, just a little. That was all that counted to him - just a little love from her. That would make his life bearable. It would give him a reason to keep breathing.

Sam stormed across the street. He was going in. He was going to see Mai-Mai and this time she would see how much he loved her. She would want to throw away all the luxury and come back to a man who really loved her, a man who was not out for the superficial, but offered the significant. She was going to see the light. Yes, she would finally realize the love she had tossed aside for the frivolous emptiness that she was now embracing.

As he flung open the glass door to the building, he was immediately stopped by the burly doorman who grabbed him and quickly pushed him to the far wall. As he did so, another menacing looking solitary figure walked into the building behind him unnoticed as he pushed the elevator button and casually escaped the eyes of the two men who were engaged in a pushing match. The doorman, pinning Sam by leaning his broad shoulders against his chest said. "You have been told Mr. McCloud; you are not welcome in Mrs. McCloud's apartment. She left strict orders for you not to be admitted. I am just doing my job. Please don't be difficult. You must leave."

Hopelessness overwhelmed him, and in his drunken state, he was in no position to argue with a physically superior man. He bowed his head in disgrace and started to leave. As he got to the door, he turned and bolted toward the elevator. The doorman pursued him, grabbing him by the arms and pinning them behind his back as he ushered him out, not bothering to notice one man who exited the building behind them. As he stood on the street arguing with Sam, who was pleading for entry, about one minute later, another man exited behind the two who were now drawing a crowd of on-lookers. One of those watching the fray shook his head and said, "Go home and sleep it off bud. It's too early in the day to be this drunk."

Embarrassed at his abysmal behaviour, Sam lowered his head and sauntered off. As the doorman was walking back in, Andy Deluca, who was familiar to the doorman, as he had been a periodic visitor to Ms. McCloud's apartment the past couple of months, was given a knowing nod and offered assistance opening the elevator door.

On the way to the second floor, Andy was thinking about how mystifying it was that Mai-

Mai was interested in him. He was just a blue-collar window washer with no future, but apparently he had something Mai-Mai really liked. Yeah, he thought, what I am packing between my legs got me Chablis, and damned if it hasn't landed Mai-Mai now. Hell, I have my suitcase at her place, ready for a weekend in the Hamptons, free of Chablis for a few days. He would just tell her he was going fishing with the boys. There were plenty of his buddies to back him up. They always did. Frankly, being married to a transsexual was a bit boring for him now as the novelty had worn off after the first few months. There were only two holes to use for pleasure. With Mai-Mai, he could use all three, and really enjoy himself.

He had met her at the theatre where she was appearing in a play. He was washing windows while she was in her dressing room taking her make-up off after a daytime dress rehearsal. He had peered in at her and she obviously enjoyed it. She smiled, crossed her legs and gave him a full view of the merchandise. She even gave him a little wink. When he was waiting outside for her, she was not coy at all. She actually liked an occasional trip to what she called the wild side. When she got a look at what Andy had to offer, she decided a lower-class lover was a welcome respite from the blue bloods who usually provided her with sex that was more work than pleasure for her. Andy was uncouth, ill-mannered, even downright disgusting at times, but the sex was great. He had a huge tool and knew how to use it, and he used it often. In fact, that day when he dropped by to see her, he assumed that there would be a little rendezvous with Mai-Mai in her bedroom for a midday quickie that would allow him to go back to work with a spring in his step.

As he approached the vestibule, he noticed the door was slightly ajar. Yeah, she didn't want him to waste time opening the door. She wanted him to walk in and get down to business. He figured she would be in bed naked with her legs spread wide for him.

He walked in and noticed that the bedroom door was completely open, but no one was on the bed. Hell, didn't she know what he wanted on his lunch break?

As he moved toward the bedroom door, he noticed it. The legs were sticking out from behind the chair, and a high heel shoe was off the left foot, lying on its side on the floor. He approached the chaise lounge chair very tepidly. Stopping at the right corner of the chair, he was looking down. There was a pain in his chest. It was Mai-Mai, obviously dead. He could not help but notice the beautiful cameo broach on her blouse glistening in the sunlight that was filtering in through the partially opened curtains to his left. His first instinct was to call the police. Her phone was in the bedroom, so he wiped some sweat off his upper lip and turned toward the bedroom, moving slowly and methodically. He was unsure, but, yeah, he had to call the police. As he walked to the nightstand to pick up the phone, he could not make his hand pick up the receiver. It was as if an invisible force was blocking the path to the phone. No, he couldn't call. He had to get out of there. Then, he heard the door to the apartment slam shut. He bounded out of the bedroom. The silence was deafening.

Fearful of chasing after whoever it was, as he tried to go over in his mind what was happening, he looked down at Mai-Mai. The broach was gone and her blouse slightly wrinkled where it had been. He had to get out of there. He had to think. Yeah, no one knew he was there, no one. Oh, yeah the doorman. He felt like he was trapped. Damned if you do, damned of you don't. OK, he would just leave, waving good bye to the doorman like nothing happened. Then, he would come back later to get his suitcase, and ask the doorman to go up with him to get a suitcase that needed to be held downstairs for a man who would be by to pick it up. They would discover the body together, making it appear that the murder happened while Andy was not there. She had been smothered. Andy's finger prints were all over her apartment and there was no way he could wipe them all off. There were simply too many. Anyway there would be finger prints on the pillow used to smother her and they would not be his. Andy, simpleton that he was, had seen a television show where prints were taken off a pillow, so he just assumed that it was normal to do that. He failed to realize that it was a rarity when that happened, because latent prints tend to vanish on cloth after a few minutes. Like so many people who eschew reading to find out the real facts, he just accepted what he saw on television as fact. It was easier that way. He did not have to make an effort. Chablis would know, he thought, but he couldn't just call her up and blurt out such a question without arousing her suspicion. Time, right now, all he needed was time to sort things out.

As he left, only a few blocks away, the determined Chablis was walking briskly toward Mai-Mai's apartment. In fact, as Andy made his way back to work, they actually passed each other on opposite sides of the same street without realizing it.

What happened to Andy and Chablis, we already know, but Sam, who is a crucial part of this story, made his way to a nearby bar. He sat down at a table in the corner and began to cry. The bartender walked over and asked, you need some help?"

Sam had a look of stark terror on his face. He suddenly realized that he was never going to get Mai-Mai back. She was gone from his life for good. It was over, caput, finished. He couldn't even get past the doorman now. Looking up at the bartender, almost pleading, he said, "I need a double bourbon,"

The bartender, always wary of daytime drunks, said, "OK buddy, but I'll need to see the money first."

Sam was absolutely desperate. He reached into his pocket and pulled out the present he had bought Mai-Mai. "Here you go; I don't have any money, but take this. Please, I need to steady my nerves.

The bartender opened the box and there was the silver chain. "Real silver?"

"Yes, it is 100% pure silver. Paid $28 for it. Please."

"OK buddy, I'll take your word for it being pure silver. You better not be lying. That should be worth at least three doubles. I'll hold onto it for a couple of weeks in case you want to buy it back. I know what it is like to get the shakes. I'll bring your bourbon."

Sam had once written a song for a young girl and just gave it to her. He recalled some lines from that song:

Don't leave the world you desire high and dry.
Tell yourself to give it one more try.
Believe that you can be the person you want to be.
Believe in the kindness of strangers.
You have not lived a perfect day,
Unless you help someone
Who will never be able to repay.
The best portions of a good man's life
Are the little nameless acts of kindness and love.

Sam thought to himself that the bartender was one of those people he had written about. He was a man kinder than necessary, because he understood that everyone you meet is fighting some kind of battle within.

Downing his drinks quickly, he looked at the door to the bar and stood up, trying to muster the energy to go home, but he really wanted to go to Mai-Mai. It was she he wanted to wrap in his arms. It was she who had torn out his heart, stomped on it and laughed with total indifference to his pain. She had no compassion, but still he pined for her. As he struggled through the doors with his head bowed and his shoulders slumped, he said quietly to himself, "Goddamn me for loving her, and goddamn her for being so uncaring. Damn, why do I love a bitch like that?

The morning breeze slapped him in the face, but it did nothing to sober him up. He had drunk 3 doubles in less than 10 minutes. He was so drunk that he didn't even know where he was, until he took a look at Mai-Mai's apartment building and noticed the doorman was busy talking to an attractive woman outside while people were going in and coming out unnoticed. Yeah, but he had certainly noticed Sam and made sure he didn't see Mai-Mai. Goddamn him, too, thought Sam, who was in a whirlwind of kaleidoscopic fogginess that was shrouding his thinking and making him nearly lose consciousness. He was not walking; he was wobbling now, wobbling aimlessly. He was on a tightrope of despair, tumbling into an abyss of darkness. It was as if a dark hole had opened up, swallowed him and then closed up, trapping him inside.

Without Mai-Mai, Sam was as sad as a bird without wings, a lion without a roar, a violin with only one string, a piano with no keys- his was a solitary journey to the inner reaches of loneliness and despair. There was no respite from the longing for that which was now impossible. She had doused the flame and the fire only smouldered with memories of what once was and what could have been. Yes, that dark hole had claimed him now, almost obliterating his consciousness.

Only 20 minutes later he wandered back into the same bar, taking a seat at the same table, and asking the same bartender for a double bourbon as he dropped his head down onto the table whimpering. When the bartender said he couldn't give him anymore credit, a man and woman sitting beside him told the bartender to get him a drink and put it on their tab. Sam lifted his head and said, "Thanks, I appreciate that. I really need that drink bad."

The woman turned her chair toward Sam and said, "My friend, I bet you got woman problems, right?"

Sam rubbed his forehead and realized again that there were sympathetic people in the world, people who genuinely cared. "Yeah, it's been three years of despair. Three years and I am worse now than the day she left me. I won't ever get over it. It just isn't going to happen."

The woman said, as the man with her eagerly sipped on his drink and looked thoroughly disinterested, "It is hell carrying a torch. I feel for you buddy. I have been there and done that. You gotta move on."

Looking at the woman, who was in her early 40's, Sam thought that she wasn't that bad looking. Sam reached in his coat pocket, trying to find something of value to give the lady, anything. "I wish I could give you something lady, you are a kind soul."

The woman smiled and said, "You want to give me something? I am a woman who never says no. That is why I have had so much heartache." She looked over at the man she was with and continued, "I will give this guy a tumble tonight, but I will wake up alone. That's the way it is, but I am a buy-sexual. You buy me a drink and I will have sex with you, but nobody wants to stay."

Sam found something in his pocket, handed it to her and said, "That's all I got. Hope it is enough for one more drink."

She winked at Sam. Figuring the man she was with would pick up the tab for another drink; she waved at the bartender and then pointed at Sam's glass with two fingers, indicating a double.

J. Wayne Frye

Chablis: Avenging Angel for the Forgotten
In the City of Lost Hope

The church makes saints out of people like Father Sera, who used the whip to bring Native Americans to Jesus, but this kind woman was more a saint than Father Sera. She was sympathizing with a man who was down and out, lost in hopelessness. She was the true Christian who understood a drink for a desperate, heartbroken man was the supreme act of kindness. He didn't need prayers or a bible. He needed a shot of bourbon.

Fast Forward

Chablis had accepted the fact that Andy would have to spend time in jail. He still had never really levelled with her about Mai-Mai, always saying that they were just acquaintances, and that nothing was going on between them other than just friendship. Yet, at the trial, the D.A. had produced witnesses, including the doorman who said that Andy had been up to her apartment almost daily for over three months.

Chablis, had heard of friendships, but she told Andy this one was a real corker – one for the books. Every day at lunch he visited her. She asked him if he was washing her windows every day. She knew he was lying, but it didn't matter, as she figured she owed him at least some time trying to ferret out the real killer. Besides, she had seen people railroaded by Carlton before, and she had a real hatred for him and the kind of corrupt justice he represented in a country where the rule of law only applied to the middle class and poor while those at the top got a get-out-of-jail free card. Andy was a two-timing louse, but he was innocent of murder, she knew it. The key was the missing broach. Find that and you find the killer. She'd get Andy out of jail, shake his hand and divorce the two-timing son-of-a-bitch.

She had called Aaron in Stockholm and asked if she could use his office, so now she was spending time back where she used to be the reigning queen of the mean streets in the city of lost hope. Aaron's office was in the lower East Side, near the Bowery. Aaron was an uptown private eye with a lot of uptown clients, but the clients he and Chablis enjoyed working for the most were the down-and-out dregs of society who were desperate and many times unable to pay. Aaron always said, "Charge the blue-bloods three times the going rate, so you can subsidize the poor. That is the least we can do, because the government will never do anything for those at the bottom of the economic ladder. All the good things are reserved for those at the top. It is not government of the people by the people for the people. It is government of the wealthy by the wealthy for the wealthy."

J. Wayne Frye

Yeah, old Aaron knew the real America, and he fought against the evils in it every day. Well, Chablis knew that one of those evils was men like Carlton who looked on people like Andy as just useless human beings who were not deserving of justice. She wished she had Aaron by her side, because together they were once a formidable team until she tossed her career away for what she foolishly thought was love and, of course, there was that huge tool between Andy's legs that she craved desperately. That old saying popped into her head and she even let out a little laugh, "You want sex to end, then get married." Yeah, she and Andy were lucky if they did it once a week. Chablis got a look of disgust on her face and whispered to herself, "but that bitch Mai-Mai was getting it every day from my man. If Andy wasn't in jail for her murder, I would pen a medal on the public servant who smothered the bitch."

First up was finding who the two men who had entered the building were. Andy had seen two men enter the building while the doorman was talking outside to someone. He only got a rear view, but he insisted that he could identify them if he ever saw them again. Chablis had searched unsuccessfully for months.

Chablis had been so distraught over what Andy had done that she was not functioning very well during the trial, but now she was beginning to free herself of the dependence on Andy. She was finding that old self-reliance, and there was even that confident stride to her step that had now returned. She was on the threshold of being the old Chablis Louise Chavez, and if anyone got in her way there would be hell to pay.

J. Wayne Frye

CHAPTER 6
DAMN I'M GOOD!

Chablis stood behind the glass enclosure looking at Andy, no longer with love, because he had killed that with his infidelity, but she did have pity, because she knew he was innocent. She had heard the story about why he was up there many times, but she still did not believe it. Still, he insisted on sharing it one more time. She asked herself if she could endure the lie again. Well, they were getting ready to transfer him to prison, so "why not," she said to herself.

"I know you don't believe it Chablis, dear. Hell, the damn jury didn't believe it, but it is the truth. Yes, I had my suitcase there, but it was all over. I knew it was over. She was just using me for a plaything. I was a toy, her toy, nothing more. I have been such a good husband. You know I have."

Chablis did not want to upset him since he was headed for prison so she kept her temper under control, but how she wanted to say, you have been a manipulative, controlling, lying son-of-bitch and you know it." She looked down at cell phone that he gave her to keep tabs on her, texting or calling every two hours to make sure she wasn't with another man. If she didn't answer, she was interrogated when he got home. Yeah, he was a good husband alright.

"I only went there to get my suitcase and tell her I was not going away with her. That the trip was off and I was through playing her stud."

Again, Chablis held her disdain for his explanation in check, but she was thinking to herself, "Yeah, that is why I was never getting any sex. You were too worn out from banging her."

"I realized that it was only you I loved. Damn, I was a fool" said Andy as he slightly whimpered and then continued. "I realized packing my bags and leaving with her was stupid, so I was going to get my suitcase and come home. Of course, I didn't get the suitcase did I," he said as he gave Chablis a quizzical look. "Then he wiped his brow and said, "You see, I was too frightened, too overwhelmed with fear to get the suitcase. I wasn't thinking straight. What do you do when you see a woman lying dead on the floor? You sure as hell don't think rationally."

She leaned forward, her breath causing the glass to fog up slightly. "Andy, I know you did not kill Mai-Mai, but you just admitted the truth. You were inside the apartment."

Andy hung his head and said, "Yeah, I guess I slipped up. OK, I was in the apartment, and I saw her body there. I have stupidly denied it I suppose, but I am just a poor working man being railroaded for murder. What do I know? I thought insisting I was not in the apartment was smart. I should have told the truth, but what difference does it make now?"

Chablis, a look of concern on her face, said, "You are right Andy it doesn't matter in the scheme of things. This is a city where all but a small percentage of the population have lost hope. The people like you who toil for a living are just cogs in the giant wheel of capitalism that grinds people up. However, I know Carlton never even entertained the thought of investigating other avenues that might have turned up the real killer, but you are looking at a woman who is about to become the avenging angel in the city of lost hope. I am through sitting on the sidelines of life as a result of your control. You are seeing a resurrected Chablis Louise. I am going to get you out of this jam, Andy. You don't deserve it, but I am going to bat for you, and I am going to hit a home run. No more incompetent attorneys or hoping for justice. I am going to get real justice!"

Andy stiffened his back, sat up a little straighter and said, "Damn, Chablis. You are a force to be reckoned with. I knew that the first day I met you. I am glad you love me so much."

Chablis wanted to blurt out that she had not loved him since he had betrayed her, but she wanted to give him confidence, so she kept quiet, smiled and got up. She gave him a wink and headed out the door confident that she was on her way to victory in the battle against malfeasant and shoddy police work. Her first stop would be the 23rd Precinct office of Armand Carlton.

As she left the lock-up on Lower Broadway and 33rd, she genuinely enjoyed the men staring at her. She had missed that. Andy had given her that stern look of disapproval when she showed up in high heels, a tight-fitting skirt and a low cut top exposing her small but perky breasts. He had said nothing, but she knew he was worrying that he was going to lose control of her. Hell, he could stop worrying. He already had lost control. She had declared her independence and complete freedom from the manipulation she had stupidly submitted to the very day she found out about his infidelity. She would work to free him, but when that was done, she was out-the-door.

Most transsexual women cower in the dark shadows of anonymity, fearful to tell loved ones, family, friends and colleagues who they really are. They live life in hiding for fear that discovery may cost them too much. They do not realize that keeping a dark veil of deceit over themselves is denying others the right to either accept or reject them based upon factors that are critical to self-respect. However, there are a few women like Chablis who refuse to bow before the mediocrity of deceit, duplicity and hypocrisy. These women are so courageous that they are a marvel of intestinal fortitude and bravely stand so tall against adversity that they force their loved ones to openly embrace them before all, because those who refuse to proudly proclaim their love openly for a transgendered person are themselves living in the shadows of self-doubt, hypocrisy, insincerity and deception.

Chablis was about to enter the fiery furnace of contempt at the 23rd Precinct. Like Shadrach, Meshach and Abednego in the Bible, she would be unafraid of the fiery furnace, because she had righteous indignation and self-confidence that was a mighty shield against the narrow-minded, bigoted buffoons like Armand Carlton who dared call themselves New York's finest.

She walked up to the desk sergeant who remembered her from years before. He was a nice man who had always treated her with respect. "Chablis, how nice to see you again. Sorry to hear about your husband getting such a heavy sentence."

"Thanks Sergeant Bailey. I am working on getting the real killer. I am out of retirement and ready to kick some ass."

Smiling, Bailey said, "That a girl. Don't take it lying down. You and I both know that Carlton is not the most skilled detective on the force. My guess is that you are here to see him."

"I am."

Shaking his head, Bailey said, "He ain't gonna be happy."

"Sergeant Bailey, I am not in the business of making people happy, especially Detective Carlton. Happiness is reserved for those who can afford a good attorney. Most people can't afford one."

Bailey buzzed her in and as she was walking through the swinging low gate, he pointed toward the door marked homicide. "Have a good time Chablis."

Bailey enjoyed watching her walk up to the door and turn the knob. Chablis looked almost as good going as she did coming.

There were four detectives in the room, and they all were familiar with Chablis, because Carlton had told them about the transsexual private eye when the case against Andy Deluca was being laid out for prosecution. All four were taken with Chablis' incredible beauty and as they stood and stared, Chablis had to admit that she was enjoying the admiration. Carlton spoke up first. "So, what the hell you want?"

"I want to catch the guy who killed Mai-Mai McCloud."

Cynically, Carlton barked, "We caught that guy. Been tried and convicted."

Chablis, a look of disdain on her face, even more cynically than Carlton, blurted out, "Been tried and convicted yeah, but you haven't caught the killer."

"Look Chablis, your husband is made to order for the killing. You can't face the fact that he was a lying, cheating son-of-a-bitch who was about to dump your freaky ass. He decided he wanted a real woman. Get over it."

Ignoring his bigoted, uninformed, stupid remark, because she didn't want to waste time educating an ignorant, unenlightened man, Chablis said, "Carlton, I have a question. You ever even bother to check Mai Mai's call records? Look at them. The sorry attorney Andy had didn't bother to introduce it as evidence after he had them checked, but don't you think it is kind of stupid for Andy to call a woman he killed after he killed her, then to come back to the crime scene to compound his stupidity?"

Carlton, shaking his head, said, "He did it for an alibi, pure and simple."

Chablis, sighing and breathing deeply, as all four men stared longingly at her braless perky breasts pushing against her blouse, replied, "You and I both know he is not that smart. I am on the case now, and I will be filing a freedom of information writ for all the evidence. The attorney went over it, but he is almost as dumb as Andy."

Carlton leaned back in his chair and said, "What the hell you want? Get to the point and then get out."

"Carlton, before you roughed Andy up, did you bother to really look around that apartment. Was there something, anything there that was out of the ordinary? I was there, but I was too distraught over Andy's infidelity to really make an intelligent appraisal."

Carlton, despite being arrogant and self-serving, seemed to be giving it some thought. While doing so, one of the other detectives, who was eyeing Chablis longingly, let out a little grin. Chablis, aware of his interest, took a deep breath to accentuate her perky nipples just to tantalize him.

Carlton, after a few seconds of thought, said, "OK, there were two things that might mean something. It changes nothing in reference to Andy's guilt, but there was a slight intention in the carpet by the chaise lounger, almost as if some person had made a deep impression of the letter M on the plush carpet. Mai-Mai had carpet residue under her finger nails, so we just assumed it was her struggling against her assailant. There was also a part of a matchbook in the doorway just lying on the floor. Nothing really important in all likelihood, just probably dropped by Mai-Mai, as she was a smoker. All those things are insignificant when stacked up against your husband's presence there."

Chablis said, "Thanks a lot Lieutenant Carlton. You just never know do you? I saw the matchbook, but didn't figure it was significant. The part I took had on R on it. Anyway, if a competent detective was on the case, those things would have been explored. I was too traumatized to investigate things properly, but that is behind me now. I am going to makeup for your incompetence, starting today."

Carlton, his back stiffening and his look growing sterner, his demeanour more arrogant, pointed his index finger and waved it furiously at Chablis as he leaned forward and said with an air of disdain, "You are messing with dynamite and it will explode in your face. You are a fucking freak of nature bitch looking for trouble."

Chablis Louise Chavez looked at police Lieutenant Armand Carlton with her dark brown eyes sparkling with that usual "I don't give a damn attitude" that seemed to bore a hole right through you and penetrate your soul. "You call me a bitch and think that insults me. Hell that is a compliment. That means you look at me as a woman, and I am more woman than any man in this police department can handle."

And what a woman she was. Standing 5 feet 6 inches in her 3 inch heels, her magnificent, perfectly formed perky nipples jutting out like two small mountain peaks, her tight-fitting blouse hugging her midriff just enough to show the taunt, rippling abs that pushed at the garment with each breath she took, her jeans forming a sensuous curve around her hips and those long lithe legs leading down to her gorgeous feet and the perfectly pedicured toenails with bright red nail polish glistening in the pale light of the squad room made her look like dynamite that might explode any minute.

Lieutenant Carlton, clinching his right fist, leaned forward over his desk and said, "I don't need this Chablis. You caused enough trouble around here when you were gumshoeing with Aaron Adams. We were glad when you retired and got married. We have the right man. We know it, because every piece of evidence points to Deluca. So, he is your husband. So what, that does not make him something special. First, in my book, that makes him a goddamn queer. You are wrong. I don't see you as a woman. I see you as an abomination, a freak of nature. You should find a hole and crawl in it, pull the earth over you and hide your despicable self from the world. Your kind is ruining the moral fibre of this country.

People like you are disgusting. Get the hell out of my office, and do us all a favour – get the hell out of New York City."

Chablis smiled the smile with all those glistening, sparking white teeth showing, shining brightly in the dim-lit squad room as Carlton and three other detectives all had arrogant smirks on their faces.

Taking a long, deep breath and sighing, Chablis, in her soft melodic voice that usually sounded like a nightingale, but in this instance had the screech of a crow, said, "Listen you son-of-a-bitch, I know what all four of you homophobic bastards are thinking. You all look at me and get a tingle between your legs, because I am more beautiful than any woman any of you has ever been with. You cover-up your desires by berating that which you are too stupid to understand. I may have a dick between my legs, but I am more woman than any one of you can handle. You are ashamed to admit it, but I know all of you would love to have me wrap my gorgeous puffy lips around those puny things between your legs that you think makes you men."

Then she turned around, and purposely accentuated the sway of her hips to titillate them with her voluptuous ass as she walked provocatively toward the door, and looking back over her right shoulder, said, "I have sucked bigger lollipops than what you bastards have to offer."

On the way out Chablis gave Sergeant Bailey a wink and said, "Left Carlton with egg on his face."

Bailey winked back and buzzed her through, thinking to himself, "Damn, what a woman!"

As Chablis walked down the street filled with people seemingly lost in the thread of daily survival, she noticed how forlorn so many looked. The majority of people were not living. They only existed, struggling to get through another day in a world that was making them all slaves to the corporate bottom line. Yet, they embraced their slavery and warmly wrapped themselves around an idea that had been bankrupt long ago. America was not a nation any more. It was a giant holding company for the corporations that pulled the strings. Chablis and Aaron Adams were anachronisms in a world that had lost its bearings, a world where there was no moral compass any longer. In the name of greed, all things were possible. Even the church, with its hand out for donations and its business-like operations, was nothing more than just another corporation out to milk the people dry.

As she wandered aimlessly toward the Leslie Howard Theatre in lower Manhattan she thought about what Andy had told her. Hell, it was mostly lies, but still she could not help but wish it was the truth. The biggest lie was his insisting he was going to Mai-Mai's to break up. Yeah, sure. She could hear his pleading with her when he was trying to justify being at her apartment. "I couldn't just up and leave her with no explanation. She didn't deserve that. I tried to reach her on the phone a couple of times, then I just decided to go up. I don't expect you to believe me; I wouldn't blame you if you didn't, Chablis. I was not going to go away with her. Hey, I am lucky you will tolerate me. I am not the kind of guy who attracts classy dames and I know that. You are the only woman with class who is willing to have anything to do with me. I know I am a loser. Hell, I know you think I am a loser, but you love me, so you stay with me."

Yeah, thought Chablis, you are a loser, but the biggest thing you have lost will be me when all this is over.

Life Was Like That

Chablis had wallowed in unmitigated misery for far too long, crying over a lying, cheating man who did not deserve her tears. She had always been such a strong-willed woman, but something inside her disappeared when she met Andy. She lost that old self confidence as she fell prey to his manipulative nature that was as smooth as polished steel. He was horribly uncouth and unsophisticated, but he had a shy, "ah shucks," good old boy charm that melted Chablis' heart and made her throw away a successful career and a bevy of eligible bachelors. She even ignored the advice of the man who probably cared as much about her as any man she had ever met. Aaron Adams was like a father to her, but like a wayward child, she refused to listen to his warnings about where a relationship with Andy would ultimately lead. Andy had actually kept himself in check, more out of fear of what Aaron might do if he abused her than anything else. Aaron was Chablis' ace-in-the-whole. Andy lived in mortal fear of the man, and he hated Aaron intensely, even going so far as to contemplate how he might kill Aaron and finally be able to exert unencumbered control over Chablis without fear of retribution.

Well, now Chablis was actually beginning to get free of Andy's vice-like control, only Andy didn't know it yet. That realization would come when Chablis found the real killer and Andy walked out of jail a free man. That would be the day Chablis also walked free. Andy was about to have a rude awakening, and it would not be pleasant.

Things could never look so dismal to her again. You can only cry in despair and misery so much. She was done crying over Andy. Now her only tears would be for Andy and his predicament that was predicated on his being among the underprivileged class which never received any justice. However, she would put those tears for Andy aside, too, as she embarked on a journey into that city which so captivated her, but also brought her great consternation for its lack of compassion and concern for those who toiled in obscurity to make it function. She felt a surge of Dicksonian disgust for the stark contrasts between the affluence enjoyed by those in Uptown Manhattan and those who had to live on the periphery of affluence struggling day to day and those who were permanently consigned to poverty in the bowels of the city.

Journeying through the bowery, she observed with procession the dingy hue of every object around her. She was appalled by the murkiness, the hopelessness etched on the faces of the nameless thousands huddling in doorways and vacant lots and a pall hung over the place, as if the sun never shown through the clouds of despair that kept the people imprisoned in misery. The streets were thronged with working people on their way to the homes of the affluent or to the corporate headquarters where they toiled for meagre wages in service to the rich. The hum of the working man resounded all about as the silent cries of wretchedness and tribulations were the heavy burdens that stooped the shoulders of those who were being ground up by the machinery of capitalism. Theirs was the lot of the working class in service to those at the top of the economic ladder.

Chablis: Avenging Angel for the Forgotten
In the City of Lost Hope

Chablis began to see a gradual change as the dark pall of misery slowly subsided as she entered Soho, a neighbourhood in Lower Manhattan filled with artists' lofts, art galleries and trendy boutiques. The area was a history lesson as an archetypal example of inner-city regeneration and gentrification, encompassing socio-economic, cultural, political and architectural developments that crowd out the poor to make room for those up and coming entries into the stratified atmosphere reserved for the moneyed class. The only poor in Soho now were those who worked there but could not afford to live there.

On Main Street was the Leslie Howard Theatre, named in honour of the great British actor, perhaps best know for his portrayal of Ashley Wilkes in *Gone with the Wind*. The large ornate doors were locked, so Chablis went around to the back of the theatre where she entered through a metal door that led to the rear of the stage. There was no one about, so she took the spiral staircase up to the second floor and strolled down the gangway that seemed to tetter precariously along the edge of the building until she got to a large room at the end. The sign over the archway caught her eye: *Through these portals walk those who lift characters from paper and give them life.*

Yeah, thought Chablis, and just maybe someone lifted a murderous character from a page and killed Mai-Mai. Perhaps there were those who wanted her out of the way. Maybe someone who thought they might have a shot at the role she was playing or someone carrying a grudge.

A short chubby man in his 50's was sitting behind a desk and asked as Chablis walked in, "Can I help you lady?"

Chablis, flashing that incredibly disarming vibrant smile that melted men's hearts and made them pant like a long-distance runner just finishing a marathon, said, "I am in search of some information on a woman who was an actress in several plays here. I was wondering if you might be able to help?"

The man gregariously replied, "Been here ever since the place opened over 45 years ago. What's her name?"

"Mai-Mai McCloud."

"Knew her well," he proudly boasted and continued, "She was not the most popular actress around. Could be a real pain if you know what I mean. One of those actors who thinks they are something special."

Chablis smiled as she said, "Yeah, I know a lot of people like that. It is not just actors who can act that way. So, was there anyone in particular who had a grudge against her?"

"Particular? Hey, everyone had a grudge against her, even me, but there was one guy, Danny Burroughs, who almost got into a physical altercation with her, right about where you are standing. It happened two days before her death. If she hadn't been knocked off, Danny and she might have killed each other right here in the theatre eventually."

Chablis, in her soft, melodic voice that seemed to be in an echo chamber because of the immensity of the room, said, "Hated each other, uh? Sounds pretty serious. OK, but why?"

"Seems at the morning rehearsal that day, Burroughs, who is the stage director here, had a set boom lowered during the dress rehearsal. That is a no, no in the theatre. It distracted Mai-Mai and she stormed off the stage, went right in here, back to Mr. Donaldson office," he turned and pointed at Mr. Donaldson's office as he continued, "and I could hear her screaming about what happened. Mr. Donaldson tried to calm her down, but she was having none of it. I heard him even threaten to fire her, because he was tired of her being such a Prima-Donna. So, she stormed out of his office as Burroughs was coming in here to apologize, but before he could say a word, she was in his face wagging her finger and telling him how unprofessional he was. She was yelling right in his face like a wild woman. So Burroughs is almost ready to slap her across the face when Donaldson walks in from his office and separates the two of them and orders Burroughs out of the office. Burroughs said, 'I'll get you bitch" and left. Meanwhile, Donaldson tells Mai-Mai that her gig here is up as soon as the play closes. Mai-Mai says, 'I got a contract and storms out. Donaldson shouted 'there are ways to break contracts,' looked at me kind of dismissively and walked into his office."

Chablis, heartened that there were others who could be suspects in Mai-Mai's murder said, "Did the police question you?"

"Sure, I talked to a Lieutenant Carlton. He didn't seem too interested."

"He wouldn't be I am sure. So, is Mr. Donaldson in?"

"Sure, I will buzz him, just a minute."

A red light flashed on above Donaldson's office, and the chubby guy, pointing at the door, said, "Go right in lady."

Donaldson was a very handsome man, probably in his late 50's, but he had an air of sophistication about him that even made young women like Chablis think that it would be nice to wrap yourself in the arms of this white haired gentleman for a few hours of adult fun between the sheets.

His voice was deep and seemed to resonate with authority. "So young lady, may I be of some assistance?"

"You can sir. I am Chablis Louise Chavez, a private investigator looking into the death of Mai-Mai McCloud."

In a somewhat stern tone, Donaldson replied, "I was under the distinct impression that her killer had been caught, tried and convicted. At least that is what I heard on the news.

"Well, someone certainly was. In fact, that someone was my husband, but they convicted the wrong man because of shoddy police work. I am here to right an injustice."

Donaldson rubbed his chin and said, "I appreciate your devotion and determination Ms. Chavez, but I am not sure I can help you in anyway. Mai-Mai came to work for the theatre awhile back. I will be frank. She was hired because I had a tryst with her, but that was not the only reason. She was actually a pretty good actress, all things considered, able to play many roles. She was a natural for a repertory company like we have here. However, she had serious problems with other actors and the crew right from the beginning. She was a bit high strung and seemed to think of herself as a star. Well, she was a star, but Soho is a long way from the bright lights of Broadway. She was just an above average actress who would never have made it to the uptown theatres. She knew it, but didn't want to face reality."

Chablis was impressed with Donaldson's candour, and noticed he kept eyeing her perky nipples that pushed tantalizingly against her blouse. "I understand there was a big argument between a Mr. Burroughs and Mai-Mai."

"Yes, it became so heated I had to break it up. However, Burroughs was only one of many Mai-Mai ticked off with her arrogance."

Quizzically, Chablis said, "You mean there were others?"

"Yes, I was probably one of the worst. She and I were always at odds. Makes me a suspect I suppose?"

Smiling, Chablis said, "It does, but don't take it personal."

Donaldson, now thoroughly, unabashedly and overwhelmingly enamoured with the alluring Chablis, said, "I won't, Ms. Chavez."

Chablis, sensing that she could use her feminine wiles advantageously, said in a low husky sexy voice, "You can call me Chablis, Mr. Donaldson."

Now, he was being sit up for manipulation. He replied, "I am Tom."

Chablis, looking seductively at him with the full knowledge that all men were suckers for her coy sexuality, said, "Well thanks Tom. I am so pleased that you are eager to help. You would be surprised how difficult it is to get information out of people. I suppose you could supply me with the names of a few people who might be suspect in Mai-Mai's demise."

"I could do that," he said as he moved back behind his desk, still not taking his eyes of Chablis even as he sat down and began to scribble some names on a small pad of yellow-lined paper, "and I will explain each name to you."

Chablis, moving beside his desk slowly and provocatively, leaned over and closely watched as he finished writing the first name with some difficulty, because he was following her movement toward the desk with obvious relish. Chablis couldn't see it, but she had been in those situations too many times not to know that Mr. Donaldson was, no doubt, getting a huge erection.

It had been so long since she had enjoyed her sexuality the way she was savouring it with Donaldson, because Andy had always kept a tight rein on her. Well, that was over now. Andy had cheated, and Chablis thought that if she had the time, she would repay his infidelity ten-fold, but for now, she had to restrain herself. There would be a day for that, but this wasn't it.

Donaldson was having difficulties keeping his composure as he was overcome with desire for exotic, alluring Chablis. The sexual tension was so thick you could have cut it with a knife. He looked up at Chablis as he pointed down at the first name on the list. "So, you already know about Danny. Then there is Marcus Ruffalo. He owns the Top Hat Club in Manhattan. A real old-fashioned top-hat and tails type place. He is a real dresser, thinks he is dandy. He was always hanging around here, making himself a pest if you ask me, bringing Mai-Mai flowers many nights after the performance. She did leave with him many evenings. However, once, in fact, three or four nights before her death, when she left with another man and he was just standing in the wings with a dozen roses in his hand as she walked by without even giving him a glance, I heard him say to Danny who was there, 'damn bitch, she'll get hers, just wait and see.' He was staring daggers as she went out the backstage door."

Donaldson could smell the scent of lilacs on Chablis, as she always dabbed just a small bit of Midnight Enchantment perfume right under her chin. The smell was intoxicating and making the problem in Donaldson's pants worse. He could barely compose himself.

Looking up at her longingly, he said, "and there was Bull Benton. I am sure you have heard of him."

Chablis, now herself overcome with an intense desire to fornicate with the handsome older man, replied, "Yes, Bull is a well-known numbers runner and also operates a protection racket on the lower eastside. He is Teflon, though; the authorities can never get anything to stick. So, was he seeing Mai-Mai, too?"

"I assume he was. Anyway, he was around here constantly for a long time and left with her on occasion."

Chablis, remembering that Mai-Mai's husband, Sam McCloud had testified at the trial said, "What about her husband, Sam McCloud? He ever show up here?"

"All the time, usually drunk. He couldn't let her go. Totally infatuated. Finally, I had him barred from the premises, because he was always causing a frightful scene. He'd still hang around out on the street. Couldn't do anything about that. He was always pleading with her to come back to him, but never saw them argue. Well, him anyway, she would shout and scream at him, but he would just stand there and take it like a wimp. The man was hopelessly in love with her and she cared nothing about him. Now he is probably crying at her grave wailing away with a bottle in his hand.

Chablis moved a bit closer to Donaldson, her right breast brushing against his arm as she leaned over to look at the names Donaldson had scribbled on the paper. She tilted her head to the right a bit and smiled at him. He could feel her breath on his cheek and the erection in his pants got bigger.

Chablis looked down at his pants and said, "That all the ones who had serious trouble with her?"

Donaldson turned toward her and his lips quivered. "Yeah, that is about it," he said as he took a deep breath.

Chablis noticed his erection was obviously causing him pain. She smiled at him again, turned and provocatively walked over to the door and pushed the latch closed. She then turned back, and as she sauntered toward the desk smiling she moved to the right and almost whispered, "You have a serious problem there Tom. I am going to take care of it for you."

Donaldson nearly had a heart attack at the brazen behaviour of a woman who was absolutely fascinating. Chablis reached down and swivelled his chair toward her. Donaldson was almost in shock and could say nothing. He was just staring as Chablis dropped to her knees, reached down and felt his stiff member, massaging it and smiling. It had been three years since she had exhibited such brazen behaviour, but she felt no longer bound by her marriage vows. Andy had destroyed what they had, and she thought to herself, maybe his cheating wasn't all that bad, because she missed the kind of wanton behaviour she was now engaged in. Yeah, maybe Andy did her a favour.

Chablis began methodically unbuckling his pants and then skilfully unzipped them very slowly just to tantalize him. He raised his hips and Chablis pulled down his pants, stopping to carefully remove his shoes before pulling them completely off. Still, Donaldson had not said a word.

Looking up coyly, Chablis put both her hands on each side of his briefs, her long fingernails making him sigh at the touch of her softness. Again he rose up slightly to assist as she pulled down his briefs. His member sprang to attention and its enormous size sent a shiver through Chablis as she prepared to do that which made her feel like she possessed an immense amount of power over men. Yes, she could bring men to their knees with her oral skills.

Finally, Donaldson managed to utter a few words. "Chablis, don't you want to take your cloths off and we can get comfortable over there on the sofa?"

Chablis, not wanting to have to deal with explanations about her anatomy simply said, "No, you are not entitled to see me naked yet. You are lucky I am going to do this for you, and if I like what you have for me, I may come back and give you more sometime. Shut up, lay back and get ready for the thrill of your life. This will be the blowjob you will remember the rest of your life. Every one before and after will pale in comparison. I set a very high standard. Prepare to be drained so hard that you will not be able to stand up after I am through. You will sit in the chair and think you have died and gone to heaven."

All the while she was talking, she was speaking to his erect member, as if it had ears and could hear her. She blew gently on it as she kneaded his thighs, her fingers only a few centimetres from his tightening sack that housed the nectar that Chablis craved. She rolled his pants up and put them under her knees.

Donaldson was making whining noises as he sat in anticipation. Once Chablis was comfortable with her knees resting on his balled up pants, she began to play with his member, moving it up and down with her soft hands while blowing on it.

"Oh God," he said as he sighed deeply and his eyes rolled back in his head as he continued, "Your touch is heavenly."

As she worked his member slowly up and down with her right hand and fondled him with her left hand, she said, "Yes, it is heavenly, because you are with an angel of lust my dear Tom. You love my hands on it don't you?"

All he could utter was, "oh, oh."

She flipped her long, coal black hair over her forehead and let it gently brush against his member as she continued stroking it. Then she flipped it over his thighs and balls and then brought it back over his enormous erection. She paused completely and just looked up at Donaldson smiling wickedly.

For a second, Donaldson thought she was going to stop, but then she reached down and seductively pulled her dress up over her shapely hips, paused for a second and winked at him. Proceeding to raise the dress over her magnificent wash board like stomach and then over her luscious breasts that were braless made Donaldson's erection even more intense. She stood up straighter, wiggling her breasts from side to side, making them bounce seductively. Then she bent down and placed them over his member slapping at it with the yearning globes of passion.

She commanded, "Reach down and touch them, fondle my nipples properly and I will put that magnificent thing in my mouth. Come–on, you must earn the privilege of having my mouth devour you."

His eyes bulged and he let out cooing sounds like a baby as he fondled, caressed, squeezed and stroked the globular manifestations of what he thought was blissfulness as he had never experienced before. Chablis began to let out soft sighs as she savoured the power her body had over men. Her nipples became as hard as tempered steel as he tweaked them with his thumbs and index fingers.

She reached inside his muscular thighs and spread his legs. She kissed his thighs, getting close but never touching his member with her lips or hands. She made sure the kissing noises were lusty-sounding, loudly smacking her lips to affect Donaldson's sense of hearing with erotic sounds. She knew his heart was racing now in anticipation of what was coming. She could feel the blood rushing though his veins as his blood pressure was rising.

When she put his hairy sack of sensuousness in her warm inviting mouth, he let out a pleasurable moan as she swished it around inside her mouth while she stroked up and down on his member. She used her tongue to move his balls around in her mouth, her lips succulently enveloping them. All the while she continued the gentle stroking of his member up and down, up and down, up and down. The glorious ecstasy of the moment permeated throughout the room.

Now Chablis thought to herself it was time for the pièce de résistance. She slowly put the throbbing member in her mouth and his sigh was so loud that the chubby guy sitting outside must have fallen off his chair thought Chablis. She sucked faster and deeper making slurping sounds to increase his pleasure. Her intensity was furious as she craved that joy juice that made her feel all powerful when she had coaxed it out of a man. Each trip up and down his organ was a momentous journey of delight. She could feel it throbbing and shaking, so she knew he was about ready to explode.

Suddenly the contractions began with a fury and there was that reflex of the erection that made Chablis know it was coming. It was on its way up the shaft. Then the explosion came with a frenzied ferocity. She bobbed her head up and down, swallowing with gleeful delight. Donaldson let out a long, slow moan and his muscles all seemed to relax.

Just when she thought it was over, like an earthquake, there were aftershocks, and more of the liquid lust spurted out. Chablis bent down and devoured his member again so she could taste his essence. She lovingly blew on his now exhausted member and kissed the tip. Donaldson was in a complete state of exhaustion. Chablis said nothing. She got up, gave him a wink, pulled her dress up while smiling intently down at Donaldson who was so thoroughly exhausted he could not utter a word.

Smiling, she said, "Be a good boy and I might give you even more next time. I bet you are a man who really loves going in the back door. Next time I will take off my panties and give you the surprise of your life."

Donaldson seemed to be struggling for words, but they would not come. He was exhausted, but it was the best exhaustion he had ever felt. He could not find any words as Chablis unbolted the door, and walked out.

She stepped through the doorway, and the chubby clerk, grinning like a teenage boy who had just seen his first tit, looked up at her longingly, almost as if he were sporting a tremendous erection behind that old worn out oak desk. Obviously, he had heard what was going on in Mr. Donaldson's office and was wishing he could share in the fun.

Damn, Chablis thought as she sauntered through the room with head held high, shoulders thrown back and chest stuck out. This guy needs a blow job, too, but I don't have time to take care of everybody who needs one. Too bad she though. He is kind of cute.

She winked at him, grinned and said, "Got any oxygen?"

With a quizzical look, he replied, "Actually no, don't think so."

Continuing to walk away from him, she looked back over her left shoulder and said, "Then you may need the paramedics, because when I give a blow job, it is a unique life-altering experience that sometimes requires hospitalization. Be a good boy and check on your boss. Chablis Louise Chavez has left another satisfied customer exhausted and spent with delight from a mind-blowing experience. Damn, I am good!"

CHAPTER 7
WHAT A WOMAN

Chablis went home, sat at her living room desk and contemplated. She had enjoyed her sexual tit-for-tat that let her get back at Andy for his infidelity. She silently vowed that it would not be her last act of infidelity. Hell, she owed him no loyalty any longer. He was lucky she was devoted enough to continue trying to get him freed for a crime that he did not commit. Lesser women, she thought, would have simply said, "To hell with him."

Reflecting back on what Detective Armand Carlton had said about the matchbook, she reached down and took out the yellow pages. Out of instinct, she scanned the night club categories. There were many listed that started with an R, but one had an ad on the page, and the R used the same fancy script that she saw on the matchbook that day she was in Mai-Mai's apartment – *Rathskeller Club*.

Then, Chablis, staring out the living room window at the building across the street, which she often did when thinking, remembered the powder compact that Andy had in his pocket. Yeah, it had been given to Mai-Mai by some guy named Allen. That was another lead she would have to follow up. There was a guy named Allen out there who might be connected in some way.

Suddenly, she remembered there was something about the torn matchbook that she had forgotten. Yeah, inside the cover was another letter, just one letter, an M. Could it mean Mai-Mai or could it mean someone else?

That initial was somebody else's, definitely. Chablis just knew it. There was no doubt. But why would anyone put an initial on the inside of a match cover? It stood for somebody else whose name began with an M. Yeah, just maybe both names, hers and her killer's, began with the same letter.

There is always some overlooked thing, some mislaid item that is put away and forgotten. Chablis had not worn her coat for months that she had on the day she went to Mai-Mai's. In a flash it came to her. Yes, it was the address book. The address book would have some M's listed. She went to the hall closet, found the coat tucked away hanging way back against the wall and felt inside the pocket. There is was. She opened it at the M page and just stared at the listings. Maybe she was looking at the killer's name she thought. The name is in this book, if not under an M, somewhere else it was lurking, waiting for her to find it. Ah, Mai-Mai had a unique way of listing the names. Rather than putting them by the last name, she listed them by the first name, so under M's were:

Marion Bolton 212-483-2828

J. Wayne Frye

Chablis: Avenging Angel for the Forgotten
In the City of Lost Hope

Marvin Cavaletii 212-765-3455
Morton Dalton 212-765-0848
Martin Delman 212-845-8888
Mark Fitzgerald 212-345-7646

The Meeting

He was a man of integrity who was a good friend of Aaron Adams, but had been on special assignment with Interpol when Andy had been arrested and tried. John Havoc was now back in New York at his old job as head of internal affairs, the most deplorably despicable job in all police departments, because you were thoroughly hated by your colleagues, who looked upon you as a turncoat, because you were sworn to ferret out the bad apples. It was a thankless job, but John Morton Havoc embraced it wholeheartedly because it gave him purpose. He genuinely believed that the police were there to serve the public, not harass them. He also believed, like Aaron Adams and Chablis, that justice was elusive for all but the wealthy, so they were all three kindred spirits in pursuit of fairness.

The woman who was at the internal affairs desk looked with disdain at Chablis, no doubt because she resented the magnificent beauty who was taking away from her own charm. The secretary was used to attention from all the men in the office, but with Chablis standing there, they all quickly forgot the secretary, because Chablis gave off a sensuality that seemed to bounce off the walls and give instant erections to all men in her presence. The men nearly bumped into each other getting to the swinging latched gate that led into the squad room. Three of them said at the same time. "Can we help you ma'am? "

Chablis replied, "Well, yes you can. I would like to see John Havoc on an urgent matter."

The tall handsome muscular one seemed to immediately take over as he swung the gate inward and said, "Come in ma'am, I will see if he is available."

Chablis, tilting her head slightly to the right and letting her hair fall proactively over her right eye, said in her husky melodic voice, "Tell him Chablis Louise Chavez would like to speak to him."

Telling her to take a seat while he announced her presence to John Havoc, as the officer knocked on Havoc's door, the secretary was now really fuming, as all the men's eyes focused on Chablis as she sat, crossed her legs and allowed her dress to hike up around her mid upper thighs, exposing legs that seemed to go on so far up her torso that you needed a road map to navigate them.

The muscular one came back out of Havoc's office with a sheepish grin on his face and said, "Come right in ma'am."

As she got up, all eyes, even the pretty secretary's, were intently focused on her. She said in an incredibly provocative way that seemed to be an invitation to explore the delights of her womanliness, "Well thank you. And you don't have to call me ma'am, Chablis will be just fine."

The man, stuttering, said, "I, I am Dave. Dave Caldwell, Chablis."

Giving him a half wink, she said, "Well Dave, I hope you are going to escort me in."

Again, stuttering, Officer Caldwell said, "Su-su-sure. It would be my pleasure."

As Chablis walked in, John got up, came around the desk and gave her a big hug, looked over at Officer Caldwell as he stood there staring at Chablis and said, "That will be all Caldwell."

"Yes sir," he said as he slowly backed out of the room rather than turning around, because he did not want to stop looking at the beautiful Chablis until he had to.

John Havoc, stepping back and looking at Chablis said, "Still the old Chablis, making men go a little nuts when they get around you." Then he got a serious look on his face as he continued, "I am so sorry to hear about Andy. I am also sorry that the investigation was handled by Carlton, definitely not one of the best representatives of New York's finest."

He went back around behind his desk and pointed toward he leather chair in front of it as he said, "I suppose Chablis Louise Chavez is now back in the private eye business and ready to shake things up."

Taking a seat, she was not allowing her dress to hike up now, because she knew Havoc did not need to be cajoled to do what was right. He did, however, look surreptitiously at her to see how she was holding up under the strain, and he was impressed with her demeanour. She caught a flicker of sympathy in his eyes. She went over everything that happened step-by-step.

He heard her through. Just sat and listened attentively. There was no mistaking his expression, though. Finally she said, "wipe that doubtful look off your face John. You know me. I was trained by Aaron. I know lying to you would be a mistake. I am levelling with you. Everything I have said is the truth."

"OK Chablis. It is the truth, and so I am a bit doubtful about Carlton's competence. I am in internal affairs; I have to tread lightly when it comes to overstepping my boundaries. The case is closed, so I can't just open up the case again of my own volition."

She reached into her purse and brought out the address book. She tossed it on his desk. "I took that from the apartment. I did it to protect Andy. Figured his name in there might be detrimental to his case. I know it is suppressing evidence, but I genuinely was so distraught that I forgot about it until today."

Havoc leafed through it and handed it back. It doesn't matter now Chablis. As I said, there is no way anyone will reopen this case. I can offer you whatever assistance I can, though, within my limited scope. I will help you. You know that, but I can only go so far." He continued: "You are a great shamus who has worked with the very best in the business. You will ferret out the facts, but I am just not sure this address book or that matchbook with the R on the outside and the M on the inside are germane. Remember, she may not have put the names of everyone she knew in that address book. There could be hundreds of additional people that could be suspect and are not in there. Are all those people you mentioned at the theatre in the address book? Did you check that when you were going over it?"

Chablis not really particularly pleased with Havoc's attitude; nevertheless, controlled herself. "Yes, I know the people she was most familiar with might not even be in there. Yet, the address book and the names given to me by Donaldson are a starting point."

"They are, and if you need anything to assist in your investigation, I will help you all I can, but I will not sacrifice my pension, Chablis. There is a limit to what I can do for you. Remember the numbers not in there may be more important than the ones in there. Those she knew well, those she knew best are probably not in there at all."

Chablis, thinking about one name that was in there under the A's, said, "She knew Andy well, and his name was in there. She was going away with him to the Hampton's. So, she might put their names in there when she doesn't know them well, but she doesn't take them out when she does know them well."

"Chablis, you will not rest until you either prove him innocent or find out he is really guilty. I know you are like a pit bill when you get your teeth into something. What took you so long?"

Chablis sighed. "I was blinded by stupidity. I couldn't function for awhile, because I found out he was counting the days as they went by, crossing them off one by one on the calendar of his mind until he was going to leave me for Mai-Mai. I know she was only toying with him, but Andy is too stupid to figure things like that out."

"Go ahead Chablis. Do what you have to do. I know you are probably through with Andy, and frankly, Aaron and I both thought you made a big mistake when you married him in the first place. However, I know you are a woman of integrity and loyalty. No matter what he did to you, you will not allow an injustice to go un-rectified. That is why I admire you."

Chablis smiled. "What sort of evidence will I need to rectify things? There is no concrete proof that Andy killed her, only circumstantial evidence that puts him at the crime scene close to the time she was killed. You don't need concrete evidence in a case like this. I read the file. If I were investigating, I would probably have arrested Andy, too. All evidence points in his direction, but that does not make him guilty."

John Havoc took a long deep breath and held it for a couple of seconds before saying, "Get out of here Chablis. Get your nose to the grindstone and go to work on this. You have John Havoc backing you up at this end. I will do all I can for you. Stay in touch."

Chablis gave him a wink. "Always knew you were a right guy John. Aaron doesn't call someone a friend who is a fair-weather guy. He always said you could be depended on to do the right thing. Thanks for listening."

She was right about John. She knew that when he said, "Chablis, don't get your heart broken anymore on this thing. He could be guilty in spite of what you think. Tread lightly and always expect the worst. That way you won't be surprised."

John was a good man thought Chablis, as she exited his office, safe in the knowledge that she had an inside man in the police department.

The First Name

OK thought Chablis, I start at number one under the M's, Marion Bolton. Chablis, knowing the art of investigation, realized a personal confrontation was always better than a phone call. In person, you could read an individual's body language, see their facial expressions, and analyze their idiosyncrasies that might give you a clue to the psyche.

Marion was a man of maybe 50, give or take a couple of years either way, who lived in a townhouse on Blair Street off Broadway. This was a ritzy neighbourhood with all the customary accessories of wealth in a land where ostentatious living for the privileged class was not frowned upon but promoted. In America, if you got it, you flaunt it. It was called the land of the free and the home of the brave, but all the freedom went to those at the top of the economic ladder, and the bravery was only exacted from those at the bottom of the economic ladder. America was a land that did not practice equality. It only hypocritical bragged about its equality, when, in fact, it was the

First World country with the biggest gap between the rich and poor. So, looking at the BMW's, the Mercedes' and even a couple of Rolls Royce's parked in the driveways of the four story townhouses made Chablis reflect on how many of her Mexican brethren might be slaving away behind the golden gates of wealth in service to the rich.

As far as rich people go, Marion Bolton was a nice enough guy. Of course, looking at the gorgeous Chablis standing on the stoop in her 3 inch high heels, her tight fitting coat that hugged her generous curves and those long, sleek legs that seemed to go on forever despite her shortness, what man wouldn't roll out the welcome mat?

"I am Chablis Louise Chavez Mr. Bolton. I am a private investigator, and I would like to ask you a few questions about Mai-Mai McCloud."

"Sure, come in Ms. Chavez," he said as they went down a short hallway that had beautiful brocade wallpaper. "The maid is off tonight, but I will fix us a drink. What can I get you?"

"A club soda would be fine."

Smiling and observing her sit down and cross those gorgeous legs, showing off her muscular thighs, Bolton said, "Well, here you are, and I must say Ms. Chavez it is not often that I am blessed with such a beautiful guest. What can I help you with? Ask anything and it is yours."

Chablis, taking the club soda, looked up and smiled as Bolton backed toward a sofa where he took a seat. He leaned back and admired the fine form of Chablis. She said, "I am interested in how you knew Mai-Mai, and if there might be something that you know that was perhaps overlooked by the police, something that might help prove Andy DeLuca innocent of the crime. His conviction was based completely on circumstantial evidence. I need to find some holes in the case."

"In all honesty Ms. Chavez, I did not know her that well. Frankly, what I am going to tell you came out on the witness stand and is therefore a matter of public record."

Chablis, smiling, said, "I know how men are. You all have libido problems – way too much of it. I am not here to judge you. Too much of that is done in this country. That is why the country and this city have lost hope of ever rising above judgmental arrogance. I am here to try and put together some plausible explanation that might lead the evidence away from Andy DeLuca to someone else. Your infidelity is your problem and your wife's, not mine unless, of course, it makes you culpable in a crime. I can assure you that I am skilled at what I do. If you don't tell me, I will eventually get the information anyway. I absolutely guarantee you that I am as tenacious as a pit-bull with its teeth clamped down on something."

Chablis smiled the smile with all those glistening, sparkling white teeth showing. That provocative, alluring smile disarmed men and made them want to bow in worshipful supplication to this unique specimen of womanhood. It brought the mighty to their knees in supplication to her charms. Oh, and those dark bedroom eyes penetrated to your soul. They bore a hole in you and made you pant with anticipatory delight at what it would be like to hold her in your arms, what it would be like to plant a lingering, wet, passionate kiss on those thick succulent lips, what it would be like to make lascivious love to her and linger longingly in pure unbridled ecstasy.

Bolton wiped his brow as he gazed upon that which aroused his prurient instincts that were such a profound part of his psyche. "OK, Mai-Mai and I were having an affair, but I was one of many. She spread her charms around quiet freely. She liked to dangle a variety of men, keep them hooked on her charms and manipulate them for material gain. She got a lot of gifts out of me, but never any money. I simply refused any financial arrangements, even when she threatened to go to my wife. I simply went home, told my wife about it and then told Mai-Mai to do whatever she wanted, because my wife had forgiven me. End of story."

Chablis uncrossed her legs and noticed that Bolton enjoyed the view of her inner thighs as she did so. "OK, so you destroyed her blackmail attempt with the truth?"

"I did, my wife will be home in a few minutes. You are welcome to confirm that with her. I wish you wouldn't of course, because I have been paying severe penance for my infidelity for some time, and brining it up only opens up the old wounds that are just now beginning to heal.

Chablis, actually feeling sorry for him, replied, "Don't worry, I believe you."

Sheepishly, she said, "Did you know any of the other men Mai-Mai was seeing?"

Shaking his head right to left, Bolton said, "No, she was very careful to schedule her trysts at proper intervals so the men did not run into each other, but there was one time I saw another man – just once."

"You know his name?"

Shaking his head in the affirmative, he said, "Sure, it was her husband, Sam McCloud. The guy carried a torch for her that would not go out, but it was almost as if he actually delighted in her abuse of him sometimes. He kept coming back for more of it, and believe me, she gave it to him. Just a minute."

Bolton got up, went over to a picture on the far wall, swung it to one side and behind it was a safe. He quickly dialled the combination, reached in, pulled out a piece of white standard stationary, closed the safe, flipped the dial a few times, pushed the picture back over it, walked to Chablis with his right hand holding the paper and offered it to her. As she reached up to take it, he said, "You can have it. I just kept it, because, well, I don't know why. I just did. Pitiful piece of poetry I know, but I watched Mai-Mai read it to me and she laughed, just laughed at a man who was aching inside for her. Mai-Mai was one of the damned cruellest women I have ever met. Frankly, the world is better off without her."

Chablis looked down with curiosity and began to read a pitiful piece of prose that laid bare the pain Mai-Mai had caused her husband, but he was willing to endure any pain, any indignity to stay with her. Chablis could only think to herself, "Damn, I wish Andy had loved me this much. This is a man who is overwhelmed with worship for a woman who cares nothing about him, and who looks upon him as trash beneath her feet. This is a man who begs for the taste of the whip of despair from the woman he loves."

Chablis: Avenging Angel for the Forgotten
In the City of Lost Hope

As Bolton sat back down, Chablis read on, beguiled by the pain that Sam McCloud must have been in. It was a ditty of pain and longing to be with a woman Sam simply adored.

I long to feel pain inflicted by she whom I defiled.
The sadistic kisses of her
verbal assaults are deserved.
The biting pain of her whip
is payment for my slights.
Making me crawl and beg brings her delight,
so it brings me great joy to serve her.
She teases me with wantonness,
making me shake with desire
to touch her where all men long to touch.
She taunts me with her alluring ways.
I am dancing with pain, but need it for penance.
Making me beg for the slightest pleasure,
she delights as I make
myself supine to her desires.
Use me, abuse me, defile me, make me her slave
and I shall welcome it with delight,
For I am not worthy enough to even kiss her feet.
If I lay in her lap dying, a smile will crease my lips
knowing that my last breath was in service to her,
who disdainfully discarded me like a worn out
shoe that long ago outlived its usefulness.
I am nothing, and she makes sure I know it.
Thank you. Thank you. Thank you.
I played a dangerous game
that has now damaged me and cast me
into the lair of she who shall make me

J. Wayne Frye

pay recompense the rest of my life.
I embrace the pain of she who taunts me,
because I know it is well-deserved.
Bowing to her is all I live for.
Her pleasure in dishing out pain
is my breath of life.

Looking up at Bolton, Chablis said, "This man is either hopelessly in love or a masochist, maybe both."

"Yeah, Mai-Mai just read it to me and laughed. She winked at me and intonated that I was next on her list of supplicants."

Chablis, feeling she had gleaned enough information from Bolton, got up and said, "OK, I appreciate your time. Maybe I better go before your wife gets home. You don't need me around here to arouse her wrath. You have enough trouble already."

Bolton, smiling, said, "Thanks. That is nice of you. I just have to tell you something before you leave. You mind?"

Chablis knew exactly what was coming, because she had heard it so many times before. "Mr. Bolton, you don't want to say it. The answer is no. You are an appealing man, but you have enough trouble with your wife already. Keep your pants zipped and try to corral your ardour. Anyway, I would give you a surprise that you might not be able to handle."

"For a few minutes with you, I'd risk anything. You are an incredible woman, incredible."

Chablis, tempted, but pressed for time, said, "Not today. Put a lock on your fervour for carnal pleasures. Remember, that is what got you in trouble over Mai-Mai. You might find me more trouble than you can handle."

Bolton's chest moved up and down as he let out a long sigh and said, "You are worth any amount of trouble."

Chablis smiled, turned and gave him a chance to admire her magnificent posterior as she gracefully glided out the door like a gazelle.

The Second Name

Marvin Cavalettti was next on the list. Chabliss remembered that his name had a line drawn through it. Was he crossed off Mai-Mai's list of potential victims? One thing was sure. The line drawn through it meant something, but what? The number was in the reverse directory. Why? OK, thought Chablis. What difference does it make? This one she couldn't see in person, but she gave him a call. What is wrong with a phone call she thought?

The ringing seemed to reverberate through her ear, making her think that it was an echo of doubt; doubt that there really was an answer out there.

A gruff voice on the other end said, "Hello."

Chablis replied, "Is Marvin there?"

Abruptly the voice said, "Marvin who?"

"Marvin Cavaletti."

The voice, seemingly perturbed, replied, "Lady, this is the St. Francis Hotel. Ain't nobody here by that name."

Chablis was persistent. "You recently had anyone by that name staying there?"

"Lady, I ain't no memory machine. We got over 150 people living here and they come and go. What you want from me?"

Chablis, even sensually alluring by voice, almost whispered huskily, "Come on, surely you can check for me can't you? Next time I am by there, I'll come by and plant a big wet one on you for helping me out. What do you say?"

The clerk was obviously titillated by the thought of a kiss from what seemed a seductively enticing woman, replied, "I don't believe you, but I'll take a gamble. You sound like a righteous broad. What was the name again?"

"Cavaletti, Marvin Cavaletti."

Suddenly more corporative, the clerk said, "Only been here a few months, but I tell you what I will do. I'll check the registry. Come by in about two hours and I'll have the info for you. Whatcha say?"

"I say you are a smart guy who wants to make sure I pay off. OK, I'll be there, and I expect to see the registry."

Seeming excited, the clerk almost shouted as he said, "You betcha, don't worry. I will let you look at 'um. I guarantee."

The St. Francis was a pleasant enough place, but it had definitely seen its better days. However, the elaborate trim work, old chandeliers and ornate woodwork indicated a once prosperous place that was now more the province of those who lived from hand to mouth in a city of lost hope than the choice of those who reaped the benefits of a society based on greed.

This was a place that would have a far slower and less continuous turnover than an ordinary hotel, and the guests individually would be far more likely to be known. The clerk was a skinny shell of a man, probably a drug addict, who was wasting away to skeletal form because he was just one of the countless millions who lived on the periphery of a society that had no compassion. He was one of those lost to a battle that conquered victims like America conquered other countries and subjected them to corporate control. Corporations were an addiction that gobbled up people, used them and then spit them out when the maximum benefit had been exacted. Ninety-nine percent of the people in America were victims, but they were too stupid to even realize it. Their suburban home, the two cars, the three or four big screen televisions, the yearly trip they borrowed money to take, the brand-name clothes they wore just supported and fuelled a society that proclaimed itself the hope of humanity, when if effect, it was the bane of humanity, the cancer that ate up all in its path and devoured compassion. This, thought Chablis, was the result of letting the inmates run the asylum. Things were askew and the result was a society with no hope except for those at the top of the economic ladder who got all the benefits.

The clerk was courteous when she introduced herself as the woman who had talked to him on the phone. So courteous that Chablis overlooked his dirtiness of body and clothes and tried to be as pleasant as possible. He appeared to not have had a bath in a few days or have changed clothes for a week.

"I am sorry ma'am, but there is no record of a Marvin Cavaletti. Damn sorry in fact, as I was looking forward to that kiss you promised on the phone."

Chablis smiled, bent over the desk and planted a kiss on his lips, making it quick so she did not have to smell his bad breath, as he shoved the registry toward her and said, "Damn, you are a woman of your word. Damn nice looking woman too I might add."

Smiling, Chablis said, "Well thank you. You are damn nice looking too. You sure this guy wasn't here. Maybe he signed in under another name."

"Could you give me an idea of what the person looks like," said the clerk who was now enamoured with Chablis after the kiss.

Shaking her head, Chablis said, "Afraid not, as I have never seen the guy."

"Sorry lady. Wish I could help, but without at least a description, I'm not sure I can do anything for you" he said as he rubbed his pock marked face vociferously and then continued. "I'm sorry, I'd be only too glad to help you. Maybe get me another one of them sweet kisses from you."

Chablis, never one to judge a person by their looks or their station in life, and a woman of infinite empathy for those poor souls shunned by polite society was now feeling sorry for the desk clerk and wanting to bring some joy into his dreary existence said, "Why I may kiss you anyway you handsome devil."

The lobby was filled with those dregs of society who were just hanging onto life, not living it. Chablis, her magnificent form bringing excitement to a few of the men as they all sit or stood staring in amazement, could not help but think her presence was actually creating some enjoyment in the lives of those who rarely knew any. These men were lost in a sea of misery, but they were all still men, and as such, they had the natural instincts that most men have when around a woman who possessed the charms of Chablis. OK thought Chablis, I know how to vamp men and tantalize them, how to make them pant like puppy dogs wanting attention, coo like little babies wanting to suckle on their mothers' breasts and fawn with pleading for a touch of the paradise that is within that opening in my body that can tightly grip their manhood like it was in a vice. I am all powerful when it comes to the ability to arouse passion in men and make them beg for my attention, plead to just touch me, beseech me for one glance from my dark alluring eyes and crave the softness of my thick luscious lips on their bodies. Why not? Why not she thought? Why not give these men some of that which they had lost long ago in their descent into a life of hardship, heartache and anguish?

Chablis: Avenging Angel for the Forgotten
In the City of Lost Hope

They were men who had somehow lost their way and in the process lost their ability to attract women like they had, no doubt, once done in their lives. They were just longing for that which made their lives exciting. Damn, she would give them a few fleeting moments of pleasure.

Purposefully jutting out her fine, perfectly formed posterior by sucking in her stomach and artfully arching her back as she leaned onto the counter and let her loose fitting blouse with the top three buttons unfastened expose her soft, silky smooth upper chest above her small perky breasts with nipples that were causing the silk like see-through material to show the darkness of her round firm nipples made the desk clerk nearly cream in his pants while the other men in the lobby were panting like a long distance runner who had just finished a marathon. The sexual tension was rising like a vapour on the hot summer air. And through it all, there was Chablis, realizing that her power was all consuming, all encompassing and all potent. She was a volcano ready to explode and spew her ash of desire all over those who worshipped at her foothills of ecstasy.

Yes, the men were enjoying it, but so was Chablis. After all, she was a woman. Why shouldn't she enjoy vamping men, and these men had not been vamped in so long that they had given up on lust, thinking their situations had replaced lust with wretched distress. What was wrong thought Chablis with giving these down and out men who had lost their way a bit of excitement in their squalid lives of gloom that trapped them in perpetual misery. She was a vixen, a shrew of salacious merriment that offered them a brief respite from the hardships of surviving in a society that had no heart, no compassion, no mercy and no sympathy for the least of its citizens who dwelled in what had become the city of lost hope.

These men were all enthralled and captivated by the charms of a woman unlike any they had ever encountered in their lives. Standing only 5:3, but 5:6 in the three inch hills she was wearing, Chablis was making these men's spirits soar and she felt like for one brief moment she was tackling the misery caused by a society with no core, no hope, no direction. Yes, she, Chablis Louise Chavez, was an avenging angel for the forgotten in a city of lost hope.

The Revolving Door to Hope

The clerk was so enthralled with Chablis he was almost begging with his eyes for her to stay and allow him to look at her some more. The other men were captivated by every little movement she made, almost as if their lives were hanging in the balance. Chablis, almost whispering, said to the clerk, "I am really stymied I guess."

Then, something occurred to her. Could the registry be like Mai-Mai's address book, could a man's name be recorded alphabetically by first name rather than last. She hurriedly picked up the registry, flipped to the M's and there it was about half way down, "Marvin Cavaletti. She turned the register around and shoved it in front of the clerk's bewildered looking face. "There it is. He was here. Surely, you can remember him. Think hard, think real hard."

The clerk desperately wanted to remember him, because in the back of his drug-soaked mind he was thinking about another kiss from those succulent lips.

He pondered in thought, as he seemed to have wheels spinning in a head that had long ago squandered what brain power was there on drugs of euphoric manifestations to escape the doldrums of his existence. Then, it came to him. "Yeah, yeah, I remember him. I remember the dude now. Sure, Marvin was his moniker- something strange about him. Room 703 just like the register says, but he didn't seem like he belonged here, seemed out of place. He always kept his head down, kinda like he didn't want anybody to see him."

Chablis, her succulent lips parting slowly and exposing her gleaming white teeth, could hardly contain her enthusiasm. "So, now you remember him. OK, he kept his face hidden, but what about mannerisms. Was there anything at all unusual about his mannerisms?"

Again, the wheels were turning in the clerk's head – slowly, but at least turning. "Yeah, he kept his head down and turned to the right so nobody sitting where I am could see his face. But there was something else."

Chablis, smiling broadly, said, "Come on man. Earn yourself another kiss.

Excitedly, he said, "yeah boy. Yeah boy! He had a funny habit of pulling his ear with his left hand as he went up toward the elevator. Like maybe something was bothering it – some kind of pain."

Chablis, never one to go back on her word, motioned with her index finger for him to lean closer. She only had to do it once.

She planted another kiss on his lips and let it linger for about 3 seconds. Why not give him a real thrill she thought. It would probably be the last time in his life any woman would kiss him, as few women had the compassion Chablis did. "Thanks dear. You've been a big help. Want to check your forwarding address book to see if there was an address left?"

The clerk, really enjoying himself now, said, "Get me another kiss?"

Chablis replied, "You'll wear my lips out."

The clerk, thrilled that any woman besides one looking for drugs would actually have anything to do with him, said, "OK. OK. I ain't pressing my luck. You been a real good sport. I'll count my blessings and look for you."

The clerk ruffled through some files and said, "Nothing here Miss. Sorry about that."

Chablis asked, "So, was he here on November 11 of last year?"

The clerk looked down at the card file, pulled out the M's since he figured it was filled wrong like it had been listed in the registry and there it was, Marvin Cavaletti checked in November 2 – December 1. He showed the card to her and Chablis knew Cavaletti had been there when Mai-Mai had been killed. Significant she thought – maybe yes, maybe no. One thing for sure, the hotel was only four blocks from Mai-Mai's apartment.

Chablis, wanting to give clerk one last little thrill in a life that had few, said, "Keep those lips puckered big boy. I might be back for another kiss one of these days."

The clerk was wiggling and gyrating in his chair with delight. He reached down, no doubt, to adjust the erection in his pants. The guy was happier than he had been in years.

Chablis turned and looked at the men in the lobby staring at her. She gave them a big smile, a wink and headed out the door with a gorgeous wiggle.

That was the most excitement the hotel had seen in a long time, and the men were still watching as she walked through the revolving door. Marvin Cavaletti was somehow connected she thought, but she had to find the guy, and she suspected the name was false, so it would not be easy.

Meeting Sam

Marvin Cavaletti? Italian? Yes. But was he really an Italian? Marvin and Cavaletti just didn't match. Was it just a name picked at random? Then it dawned on Chablis. She had seen the name before. Well, the Cavaletti part, anyway. She walked over to Mai-Mai's apartment building and stood across the street from it, glaring at the place and to her left of it another building, an office building that soared 25 or 30 stories into the Manhattan skyline. Things in your mind are often buried there, but at the right time they come out. It was the right time and the right place for Chablis. There it was. It was staring her in the face. She had noticed it the day she went to Mai-Mai's apartment. It was insignificant at the time, but now as she looked at it things began to fall into place.

Chablis: Avenging Angel for the Forgotten
In the City of Lost Hope

The building next to Mai-Mai's apartment building was called Cavaletti Towers. Marvin Cavaletti was a borrowed name, used by someone who did not want to use his real name for fear of discovery. Used by someone who had been to see Mai-Mai the day she was killed probably, because the hotel registry showed he checked in and stayed through the murder day, but if he was the killer, how did his name get in her address book with the number of the St. Francis Hotel? That was a question Chablis would have to address, but for the present, she felt proud of herself. The old instincts were really starting to come back now. Things were gradually falling into place. All those months she had been too distraught over Andy's predicament to really do anything, but now she was free of Andy, not just because he had been carted off to prison, but because she no longer loved him. He had betrayed her and she would not forgive that from the man she had loved so intently that she had given up everything for him. However, she was also determined to see justice done in what she and Aaron Adams always called the city of lost hope where the forgotten and the marginal were tossed aside by a justice system that offered no justice at all if you didn't have the power and money to make things happen. It was a city where the forgotten toiled in anonymity, while the affluent lived their lives of excess, ignoring the real workers who were the heart and soul of the metropolis. And somewhere in that city of lost hope was someone, probably very affluent,

J. Wayne Frye

because, with the exception of Andy, that was who Mai-Mai gravitated toward, who had killed Mai-Mai.

Chablis had just been strolling aimlessly down the street, but ironically, she wound up in front of the Leslie Howard Theatre. She felt a little tingle between her legs as she remembered her brief sexual peccadillo with Tom Donaldson. She smiled as she strolled around to the back door, walked in and asked a janitor who was sweeping up where she could find Danny Burroughs. It just so happened he was not a janitor after all. He was Danny Burroughs.

"Oh, Mr. Burroughs, I am Chablis Louise Chavez Deluca. My husband, Andy, was convicted for the murder of Mai-Mai McCloud, and I am trying to piece together enough evidence to at least get him another trial. Do you mind if I ask you some questions?

Burroughs barked, "Ask away my dear. Frankly, I think whoever killed her should be given a parade down Broadway for doing a public service."

"I gather that you did not particularly care for Mai-Mai."

Shaking his head right to left vigorously, Burroughs replied, "No, I detested her, as did most of the other people here who had to endure her tirades, vindictiveness and arrogance. She thought she was a star, but was too arrogant to realize this is not Broadway. This is the end of the line for actors"

"Was there anyone who ever threatened her," said Chablis.

"Yeah, take your pick. I was one of 'um who threatened her several times. Didn't mean anything by it, and that cop, what's his name, Armand Carlton, he checked me out. I have an iron glad alibi for the time when she was killed. I was right here and there were about 10 witnesses to prove it."

Chablis, giving him her disarming sanguine, assuring smile said very calmly, "Oh, Mr. Burroughs I am not questioning your credibility. I am only trying to find something that the police might have missed."

Looking at Chablis with eyes that were dancing with lust, he said, "I understand. Believe me, I know that the police are as crooked as most of the people they arrest, so I can understand you questioning their competence. I do all the time. Been rousted and harassed by them a few times myself. This is a country where the police keep order for the rich; making sure us poor slobs stay in line."

Chablis: Avenging Angel for the Forgotten
In the City of Lost Hope

Chablis, who was impressed with Burroughs' perceptiveness on the state of affairs when it came to justice, said, "Agreed. That is why I am working diligently to try and get a bit of justice for my husband. He was just a poor working man trying to make ends meet, so he is not given the benefit of the doubt like an affluent person would be. I wonder if you could maybe tell me about anyone else who might have had it in for Mai-Mai, anyone who showed up here often, just hung around."

Burroughs pointed to a chair, indicating that Chablis should take a seat. He pulled up a chair across from her and obviously enjoyed watching her cross her legs. Of course, Chablis was not above using everything in her arsenal of sex appeal to get what she wanted from men. Her long, cascading hair that flowed like a river of desire was frequently brushed back with her soft, dainty hands that all men wanted to feel stroking their bodies. Her dancing bedroom eyes were flush with sensuality. Her pouty, moist, succulent lips that seemed to beg for a kiss were purposely licked by her tongue that she let linger on them just a second so the observer could imagine what it would be like to have it plunge into the mouth and dart about. Oh, but her legs. Her toned, smooth legs glistened like fine silk and the muscular calves flexed with just the right amount of tenseness that made men dream of having them wrapped around them so she could pulled them deep inside her, imprisoning a lover in their vice-like grip. Her legs were simply the greatest asset in her armoury of sexuality. They offered a reassured pleasurable treasury of delight, a brilliance that seemed to sparkle like a diamond.

Letting Burroughs get an eye full before continuing, Chablis smiled as if to let him know it was alright to look. After all, she enjoyed being looked at as much as the men enjoyed looking at her. It gave her an immense sense of power. Softly she said, "Mr. Burroughs, if I could get your attention on the matter at hand, I would appreciate it."

Burroughs, somewhat discombobulated, said, "Oh, oh, I am sorry. Forgive my rudeness. You are so beautiful."

Chablis grinned and replied, "It is OK." And then she played her feminine wiles for all they were worth, as she manipulated him with words as well as physical attraction by adding, "I enjoy it when a handsome man like you looks at me. It is a supreme compliment."

Burroughs was now fawning over her, ready to give her whatever she wanted. He was practically begging to help her. "You know there was one man named Marcus Ruffalo – he owns the Rathskeller Club here in Soho, who was always in here, bringing her flowers, chocolates. He was a slimy kind of guy, but she was obviously manipulating him. Then there was Morton Dalton. He is a ham actor who probably had his last part back when most movies were done in black and white. Couldn't ever figure out what he was hanging around her for, but she apparently was using him for some purpose, though. If Mai-Mai couldn't use you, she discarded you. That is the kind of woman she was."

"Know where I might find this Dalton?"

"Sure. He stays at the old actor's home right here in Soho. You know where it is?"

Chablis, nodded in the affirmative and in a very deliberate tone, said, "what about a man named Martin Delman?

Almost laughing, he replied, "Sure, he was a friend of Ruffalo's. He is his manager at the Rathskeller. He was often hanging around when Ruffalo was here, but don't think he showed her any interest for fear he might upset Ruffalo. Ruffalo is known as a ruthless man."

Chablis was on a roll now, so she could not resist blurting out, "Mark Fitzgerald, ever hear of him?"

Nodding his head affirmatively, Burroughs replied, "You can cross him off your list. He was a low-life hustler who used to run numbers before he crossed the wrong guy and got bumped."

Chablis leaned slightly forward in her chair and said, "Bumped by whom? Any ideas?"

"Of course, everyone knows it was Marcus Ruffalo, but, believe me, there is nothing that will connect him to it. He is too smart for that. Way too smart."

"OK, very helpful. Just one more name I want to run by you," Chablis said as she uncrossed her legs and gave Burroughs a full view between her legs, exposing the inner thighs that led to what Burroughs assumed was the moistness of paradise, "Marvin Cavaletti."

Almost laughing, Burroughs replied, "He is a dive bar piano player? He works up and down the Bowery in any dive that will hire him. He is a hopeless alcoholic. Used to be a pretty famous piano player in the high-end clubs. Back then he went by the name Sam McCloud."

"Cavaletti is Sam McCloud?"

Shrugging his shoulders, Burroughs said, "Sure, his appearance has changed so much, you know, all haggard and thinned out from alcohol, that he no longer looks nothing like Sam McCloud anymore. Like so many entertainers, he goes from the high-life to the slums and then is forgotten. He was eventually barred from admittance by Mr. Donaldson at Mai-Mai's request, so he took to just hanging out on the streets. Nothing Donaldson could do about that. I felt sorry for him, carrying a torch for a bitch, excuse my language, like that. She treated him worse than a junkyard dog, and he just kept coming back for more abuse."

Chablis slowly rose from the chair, her short skirt clinging seductively to all her curves, her chillingly glorious luscious lips glistening in the soft light of the hallway and said, "Any idea where I might find him?"

"Sure, he is pretty easy to find. He lives in the Marion Hotel over in the Bowery. Be careful if you go there. It is not a place for a lady."

Chablis gave him a little wink and said, "I'm not always a lady. Thank you so much, you have been a tremendous help."

Burroughs, now somewhat emboldened, said, "Any time, anytime at all. I don't suppose you would give a guy like me a real thrill and maybe go out to dinner with me some evening? I do know how to be a gentleman."

Smiling seductively, Chablis, always polite to those who fawned over her, replied, "I might consider it. I am still married, but only on paper.

That situation will be corrected when I find the real killer. I would be receptive now, but I am pretty tied up at the moment. Look me up in the phone book. I am still listed by my maiden name, Chablis Louise Chavez. Give me a call sometime."

Burroughs was so excited he nearly fainted from delirious delight. "You can be sure of that. I have not seen many women as beautiful as you are. You are definitely one of a kind, really unique."

Coyly thinking about her uniqueness as a woman, Chablis could not resist a little bit of personal levity. "Mr. Burroughs, if you only knew just how unique I am. I may let you find out one day. Don't forget to give me a call sometime."

As she strolled toward the door, Burroughs reached down to his crotch and adjusted his manhood that was straining in his pants as a result of an erection. Watching Chablis just walk was an experience that brought pleasure to men lucky enough to observe the gentle sway of her hips and the vibration of her ass cheeks that seemed to be a lure of delight. He imagined what it would be like to pound her into oblivion with a rear entry into paradise. "Damn," Burroughs whispered to himself, "what a woman."

CHAPTER 8
ST. CHABLIS

There are many types of pain.
The only one that medicine can't help
is the ache of a broken heart.
That's why there is alcohol and illicit drugs.

Hell was not a place in the bowels of the earth where little demons with pitch forks prick you in the ass and the hot fires scorch your skin. Hell was unrequited love like that of Sam McCloud for Mai-Mai. Hell was waking up each day with a hole in your heart. Hell was wet sheets caused by the stinky sweat of loss. Hell was knowing the woman you had dreamed would never leave you was gone. Hell was where Sam McCloud had lived for three years pining hopelessly for she who had coldly dismissed him as a useless impediment to that which she thought she wanted. Sam was colder now than when Mai-Mai was alive. Yes, he was colder than her rotting body under the frozen ground of winter. When she was alive, she hated him, but at least then he could suffer the indignity of dismissive disregard that she heaped upon him with vindictive joy. His was a blindness of the heart and soul. It was as if he had lost the glasses that let him see the light at the end of the tunnel, and when he went to buy new glasses, he was told that they no longer made glasses – blindness was now the norm– the blindness of the forgotten in the city of lost hope.

Chablis: Avenging Angel for the Forgotten
In the City of Lost Hope

The Marion Hotel was a place where the forlorn and lost congregated to suffer in loneliness. It was hope lost.

It was also a monument to anguish. It was a temple of desperation. It was a chapel of gloom. It was a shrine to melancholia.

Chablis walked into this cathedral of hopelessness and could smell the stench of sorrow and misery as if it was being baked in an oven of despair. This was the place where dreams went to die.

The sign outside the dilapidated hotel
Should have read, welcome to hell.
This was the last stop on the way to nowhere.
The people there had bought a one way ticket
To life lived in the abyss of self-doubt.
This was the cellar of misery far beyond belief,
And from its bowels there simply was no relief.

Scoring another drink was their life
These agonizing poor souls were lost in strife.
There lives had been tossed to the wayward wind,
They longed for death to bring the pain to an end.
Within the corridors there is a lonely forlorn cry.
They long for a hand up from the pain,
But nobody will play the compassion game.

Looking all about the wasteland of lost hope,
Dignity has taken a long, undeserved holiday.

J. Wayne Frye

Chablis: Avenging Angel for the Forgotten
In the City of Lost Hope

How many there would sell their soul for one sip?
The fountain of hope is dry in this place.
These people could simply not keep pace.
Yes, the sign outside should read welcome to hell.
Where hope, opportunity, charity, benevolence,
And compassion do not dwell.

In every moment death waits in the corridors of the mind to steal the breath of life and cover us with the veil of darkness. Human beings are constantly on the road to death from the moment of birth. Cells die each day as we meander down the road to the obscurity of the grave. There are some who seem to hurry down this road, embracing the coming darkness, because they have lost hope and are consumed by the flames within themselves that devour them, leaving them hollow shells who continue to breathe but do not live. The Marion Hotel was the place that embraced this misery. It was a home to those who had no hope.

In this dark and foreboding place of pain, the beauty of Chablis was meaningless, because all those dwelling there had lost the ability to see beauty. They only saw despondent desperation as they were all dead people walking.

She moved through the lobby like a spectre of loveliness out of place in a world where forlornness was eaten for breakfast, misery was served for lunch and dinner was a buffet of sorrow. The clerk, herself, a zombie of wretchedness, seemed to be in an addled, shaken state as she stared at Chablis, apparently wondering why a woman of poise and beauty like her would grace a place where beauty was as foreign as a Republican with compassion.

Chablis leaned over the counter provocatively and the desk clerk simply continued to stare, not bothering to greet her. Chablis said, "Sam McCloud please or maybe he is registered as Marvin Cavaletti."

The desk clerk, with no emotion, and not bothering to raise her head, replied, "Ain't never heard of no dude named Caveletti, got a Sam McCloud though, room 727. Can't take the elevator, it is outta order."

Chablis thanked her and proceeded up the debris filled stairs to Room 727. She knocked on the door, but there was no answer. She turned the doorknob and it was unlocked. Not wise she thought, leaving your door unlocked in a place like this, but, then again, what would anyone living in a dump like this have worth stealing? She pushed inward slightly and peeped into the room, noticing a trash laden floor with clothes and empty beer cans strewn all around. On the bed was a thin, emaciated looking man who had a three or four day growth of beard. He was breathing heavily and making a wheezing sound.

She walked into the room, looked down at the empty shell of a desperate individual on the brink of misery and felt a surge of compassion for a man who was obviously on the edge of a precipice of lost hope ready to plunge into an abyss of heartache that would engulf him and swallow him up in darkness.

Chablis instinctively bent down and began to pick up his scattered clothes and placed them on the dingy dresser by the window. It was as if she were trying to bring some order to this disordered person's life by tidying up his room. She picked up the beer cans and walked into the bathroom and after filling up the trash can with them, she placed the remaining ones in a neat row by the wall. She walked back into the bedroom and pulled up a rickety wooden chair and just sat, staring at him and thinking how a man could descend to the depths of despair like this over a woman as heartless as Mai-Mai? She did not want to awaken him, because he was, at least while asleep, free of the pain that obviously was still overwhelming him even with Mai-Mai dead. She thought to herself, "If this was the result of love, I want no part of it."

Sam lay on the bed face-down with his clothes on. He began to stir a bit and let out a mournful sigh as he rolled over on his back. He suddenly opened his eyes and a look of shock creased across his face as he observed Chablis sitting there staring at him. She said, "Mr. McCloud I assume?"

He blinked his eyes a few times and replied, "Yeah, but what's it to you? What you doing in here?"

Chablis in a very demure manner said, "The door was unlocked Mr. McCloud. I sincerely apologize for coming in, but it is imperative that I talk to you."

Looking disgusted, Sam said, "Lady the only thing that is imperative is that I get a drink and get it as damn quick as I can."

"Please Mr. McCloud, I need to talk to you about Mai-Mai."

Sam turned back over on his stomach away from Chablis and chortled, "Get out of here. I don't want to talk about her. I was damned when she was alive and now I am damned when she is dead. I got more heartache than any man can bear. Leave me alone."

"Please help me. I have to know some things Mr. McCloud. I know it is painful. I know how much you loved Mai-Mai. How much you still love her. I understand, but there is a man serving time in prison for a murder he did not commit. You can help right a wrong."

Staying face down on the bed with his back to Chablis, he said, "Stop bothering me. What you want to bother me for? Please, just leave me alone. Please."

Chablis, in a very reticent, almost pleading voice, said, "I am Chablis Louise Chavez Deluca. I was in the courtroom when you testified at my husband's trial. I specifically remember you looking at me sitting in the front row of the courtroom behind Andy when you got off the stand and walked by me. I could see that you had sympathy for me. I could see that you were a man of compassion. Come on Mr. McCloud., show me a little of that compassion I saw in your eyes that day."

He turned over, half sit up leaning on his right arm and sarcastically said, "Andy Deluca's wife. OK, so you are the one the two-timing son-of-a-bitch left home, and you want to help him. Screw him lady. What do you care about that cheating asshole."

Then he let out a long sigh as he looked at Chablis, almost like she was a work of art he was admiring in a museum. He shook his head a few times and sarcastically said, "So you are the one he left at home? Damn stupid son-of-a-bitch if you ask me. Mai-Mai was a looker, but she couldn't hold a candle to you lady. Yeah, your husband was a dumb jerk, real dumb."

Smiling, Chablis said, "You won't get an argument from me on that. Yes, he is dumb, and he is going to pay for his stupidity. I am divorcing his ass once I get him out of this jam, but for now, I need some information. Come on Mr. McCloud, help a poor girl out. I had to see you. You may give me some hope?"

"Why, because I had a wife who needed killing. Walk up and down any street in lower Manhattan and ask anyone who knew her if they miss Mai-Mai. I am the only one fool enough to miss her. I welcomed her abuse and disdain. Your husband did a job a lot of people would like to have done. Most people would give him a medal, only I am dumb enough to miss Mai-Mai."

Chablis, very seriously interjected, "The only trouble Mr. McCloud is Andy Deluca didn't do it. Andy is capable of a lot of dastardly things. He was so possessive of me I would say manslaughter might be a distinct possibility if he caught a man with me, but the murder of a woman – no way is he capable of that. He didn't do it. Come on, you are a decent man. Help me out here."

"Help you out how," replied a disinterested McCloud.

"Look, I know you carried a big torch for Mai-Mai. Surely you want the right guy caught and punished?"

Wiping a bead of sweat from his forehead, McCloud stared at her for a few seconds, seemingly contemplating what he was going to do. "OK, so I carried a torch for her and still am. That's my cross to bear. I don't need no pity, and they got the right guy. That detective was by to see me several times. What's his name, Lieutenant Carlton? An asshole, but seems like he had all the goods on your husband. I think you were scorned just like me and you can't take it. You can't believe your husband would dump a dame like you for a bitch like Mai-Mai. It happens all the time lady. Get over it. Remember Arnold Schwarzenegger cheated on his gorgeous wife to have sex with the chubby housekeeper they employed, even had a son by her. Men are weird creatures lady, really weird. We think with what is between our legs, not our head. I should know, look at me. I put up with abuse from Mai-Mai and just kept coming back for more. Even wrote a song about my masochist relationship with her. I am a loser and I know it; so did she."

Chablis, always compassionate, said, "Hey, you are a nice guy, I can tell – pretty good looking too I would guess when you clean yourself up. Don't sell yourself short."

Shaking his head vigorously, a taciturn McCloud said almost defiantly, "Come-on lady. You have manipulating men perfected to a fine art, but I have been through the mill a time or two. I don't need your pity. I am a drunk and I know it. OK. OK. What you want?"

"I already told you."

"OK. OK. The question was never asked me by the District Attorney when I was on the stand lady, so I didn't volunteer it but this will be a shocker for you. Get ready ma'am. I saw your husband go up there and he was up there for a good 15 minutes, plenty of time to strangle Mai-Mai. Face it, he did it."

Chablis, always thinking like a detective, said, "OK, so that night you were there carefully observing things, watching who was going and coming from Mai-Mai's apartment? I bet that really made you jealous, knowing all those other men were up there with her. And you never managed to get in?"

Getting a look of concern on his face, McCloud replied, "Not a chance, not a chance. She had me barred from the place. The doorman had strict instructions to keep me out. Don't push it lady. I know what you are intonating. I know where this is leading. The truth is I left and went to a bar and drowned my misery just like always. Then, I got so drunk I couldn't get back home, so I wobbled to a hotel for a few days, just laid there in a stupor, only going out to the corner liquor store to get my medicine for love sickness."

Chablis moved the old wooden chair closer until she was right in front of McCloud, crossed her gorgeous legs and said, "But why check in under the name Marvin Cavaletti? Seems that is a bit suspicious."

Sitting up, McCloud stiffened his back and said, "Suspicious? I have used that name for three years."

Chablis was trying to skilfully back Sam McCloud into a corner, corral him into a pen where he could not get out without revealing the truth. "Come on McCloud. Level with me. You are the only one who can help me. So, you used an alias, why?"

"Look at me lady. I used to be a pretty talented and successful guy until Mai-Mai put me on the ropes, even penned a few songs that were moderate successes in a few clubs. I still get a small royalty check on occasion. Then I wind up a drunk, playing in dives for pocket change. Hey, I was ashamed of myself. Why would I want to let people know that Sam McCloud was such a loser? Hey, eventually most people found out about me, but it was an ego thing I suppose. That's all, just ego."

"Is your ego why you bought Mai-Mai that broach that was taken off her after she was killed? You wanted her to wear something of yours, make you feel like you were still a part of her." Chablis leaned back in the chair and awaited his response.

Sam McCloud started breathing heavily as if some burden was weighting him down. "The broach, yeah I know it came up at the trial, but there was never any real proof she was wearing it. It was conjecture. Your husband killed her lady, accept it. He is lying to you."

Now, Chablis was boring in, grilling him, cornering him with conjecture not facts, but Sam was beginning to feel the heat. "Look, I didn't kill her. I was her floor mat and accepted it willingly just for a moment with her, a second. Call the desk clerk at the St. Francis Hotel. He will verify when I checked in. They have a date stamp that goes on the receipt copy the file. Go ahead, check it out. Go ahead. You ain't railroading me."

Chablis could be as persistent as a drug addict in pursuit of a fix. She really bore in. "Nobody's railroading you. Just admit it, you were there. I don't need a date stamp. I need you to be honest."

McCloud got up, took fifty cents in change that was lying on the dresser and motioned for her to step into the hallway. Chablis followed him as he went over to one of the last payphones probably left in New York City that had not been torn out by the cellular barons of greed who wanted to make everyone have to carry around those instruments that swallowed money like a man gobbling up a drink of water after a week in the desert without anything to quench his thirst. He picked up the directory, got the number of the St. Francis, dialled it and handed the phone to Chablis. "Go ahead; ask him to check the time stamp."

The clerk immediately recognized Chablis' sultry voice and filled with excitement and maybe even an erection, he was very eager to help. He pulled out his files and willingly verified Sam had indeed been there for a full 30 minutes prior to the time the coroner had set for the death. He always left his key at the desk when going out. But Chablis wasn't through as she sarcastically said to Sam, "The time of death is never precise, only a fairly accurate guess, but I will give you the benefit of the doubt. Maybe I should apologize."

As he walked deliberately back to his room, Chablis trailing, he said, "Lady, no need to apologize. You are fighting for someone you love, or at least used to love. It's OK."

Repentant, Chablis said, "Forgive me Mr. McCloud, please. I am sorry," then she reached in her pocket and laid a $20 bill on the dresser so he could buy a few drinks, turned and started to walk out. McCloud jumped up, grabbed the $20 and said, "Don't do this ma'am. It is insulting. I survive, not well, but I survive."

Chablis said, "I am sorry again. I meant no offence. I am not thinking clearly I suppose. I thought it might be of some help in dealing with your sorrow, but it appears that once again I did something inappropriate."

McCloud, now more comfortable with her said. "I wish I could help Chablis. Is it alright if I call you Chablis – such a lovely name?"

"Of course, Mr. McCloud."

Smiling he said, "Sam, Sam please."

There are moments when all the stars in the universe seem to be perfectly aligned. This was one of those moments as Sam and Chablis reached out to each other. This would be the beginning of a journey they would take to discover things that would unravel a mystery and bring them together in harmonious pursuit of truth.

Chablis sat down again and looked up at Sam as he sat on the bed. "I want to know the real Mai-Mai. I think I know her, but you are the expert. You are the one who would know her better than anyone else, because you were married to her. Tell me Sam, tell me about her. I want to truly comprehend what she was all about.

McCloud started out with a statement that described perfectly his predicament. "Chablis, I loved, no I still love a woman who was depraved of heart, mind, body and soul. She was evil inside. I know that, but it made, no, it makes absolutely, categorically no difference. She completely owns my heart. I hate myself for loving her, but it is better to have loved her and lost than to never have loved her at all. I live in despair because I loved a woman who was incapable of loving me, or any other man."

Chablis, who had broken many hearts in her day, but never with cruel intent, began to understand Sam McCloud, and she thought to herself, "I like this man."

McCloud continued. "She was a singer. I was a piano player and a hack writer of songs. She was trying to get into nightclubs as a songstress. We decided, no she decided to hook up with me because a piano player made her more marketable. A duo was better than a single. That is pretty much it. She wasn't above sleeping with club owners to get dates, and I just turned my head. It was only sex, and I loved her. I loved her so much that when she said we should get married, I just agreed, even though I knew she didn't love me. We were pretty successful, but she longed to be an actress, so she conned her way into a show by sleeping with Tom Donaldson. She saw him as better for her career, so she dumped me. I had outlived my usefulness. Then I spent the next few years begging her to come back to me. Stupid I suppose. I got on the bottle to self-medicate, and here I am in all my glory, a skid row has been."

Chablis was a compassionate woman whose eyes often got moist with compassion when she saw people hurting. McCloud was hurting. He was a man who had loved and lost. A man who had fallen prey to the bottle that was too often used to drown despair by those who did not realize that the bottle only offered more despair. Chablis' soft heart beat with sorrowful, sympathetic empathy for a man who was a victim of love – love for the wrong person. Hey, she was a victim, too. Sam was not Mai-Mai, but he was no prize.

This magnificently beautiful woman of both body and spirit arouse from her chair as McCloud sat with his head in his hands, almost sobbing for she whom had abandoned him for expediency. His was that lonely battle spent in the twilight of hopelessness. Chablis stood before him and touched his head. She said, "Sam, I am sorry for your pain."

> *Kind hearts are the gardens,*
> *Kind thoughts are the roots,*
> *Kind words are the flowers,*
> *Kind deeds are the fruits,*
> *Take care of your garden*
> *And keep out the weeds,*
> *Fill it with sunshine,*
> *Kind words, and kind deeds.*

J. Wayne Frye

Chablis: Avenging Angel for the Forgotten
In the City of Lost Hope

Chablis was just one person in the world, but to Sam McCloud at the moment she was the world. Lifting his head, he said, "I have waited many years to hear that. I am so lonely and lost." He began to sob and Chablis reached out with both her hands and pulled his head to her stomach.

She cradled him lightly as he sobbed and she gently stroked his hair as if she were soothing a baby. Sam was a baby to her. She felt a mother's warmth, because he needed someone to care for him, someone to show some compassion.

In life you can never be too kind or too fair; everyone you meet is carrying a heavy load, and Sam had carried his load for far too long. Chablis went through her days expressing kindness and courtesy to all she met, and she always left behind a feeling of warmth and good cheer, as she tried to alleviate the burdens everyone struggled with. She was one tough broad when the time called for it, or when the least in the world were trampled on, but her compassion was infinite for those struggling in desperation, despondency and anguish. This was a woman who could put Mother Teresa to shame.

In almost a whisper, Chablis said, "When your river of hope dries up and disappointment comes your way, it does not necessarily mean that you did something wrong, Sam. You did absolutely nothing wrong. You loved the wrong woman yes, but that is not sin. Love is never a sin. We live in a world where greed and getting what you can for yourself is considered an enviable trait. You fell prey to a woman who embraced that philosophy wholeheartedly. Unfortunately, that is the norm not the exception in today's world."

Sam looked up at her beautiful radiant dark smooth face that glowed with a celestial light of benevolent tenderness. "Chablis, I will do whatever is necessary to help you."

It was a cathartic moment for Sam. The pain slowly subsided. It was still there, but it was now held in abeyance. Chablis, the angel of light, had reached his heart. She had made him want to make himself whole again.

Sam, his eyes dry now, said, "So, you are a private eye, a shamus. Interesting. What's our first step? What do we do to prove your husband's innocence?"

Chablis tilted her head to one side and had a quizzical look on her face? "We, what do you mean we?"

"I mean that I am going to help you Chablis, if you will let me," said a determined Sam.

Chablis smiled and said, "You are beginning to question his guilt now, too?"

"Hey, I am a rummy and a low-life love sick loser. Carlton told me your husband did it, and I assumed he did because the police said he did. I just went into court and repeated what Carlton rehearsed me to say. I am not so sure your husband did it now. Let me talk to him. I want to get some answers to a few questions, and then maybe we can pinpoint where the discrepancies are."

Chablis smiled, reached out and touched his left arm. "You are sounding like a P.I. now." Then, she looked at his dishevelled condition and thought what the most polite way would be to tell him to shave, shower and change clothes. She continued, "I will wait in the hallway while you shower and change clothes."

Sam, wise to why she was nicely suggesting he do those things, replied, "You don't have to be so subtle. I know I need to bathe and get cleaned up. I know how to close a bathroom door, too. You can sit right where you are."

Chablis, with those luscious thick lips puffed out in the most alluring manner, let that winning smile slowly creep across her mouth. Even a down and out alcoholic like Sam, who had sunk about as low as a man could, was not able to resist getting a warm glow inside just looking at Chablis. She could light up the darkness with that smile, and Sam had been in the dark for far too long.

As they were going to the holding prison where Andy was waiting for his transfer to Sing-Sing Penitentiary, Chablis said, "I think the key is that broach. The cameo is the key. We find that cameo that was taken off Mai-Mai, and we find the killer. The killer was in that apartment while Andy was in the there, but he missed him by only a few seconds. The killer ran out while Andy was in there."

Sam, sitting in the taxi beside Chablis, suddenly seemed to drift off into deep contemplative thought as he sighed and looked out at the bright lights. Then he enthusiastically blurted out, "The cameo. I saved for a year to be able to buy her that, and she left me four weeks after I gave it to her. Yeah, you are right. Whoever killed her took that cameo, but why? Why would the killer take it and nothing else? There were other more valuable things in the apartment. She had a $25,000 diamond on her finger one of her tricks bought her. She had gold and silver trinkets in her bedroom. Why the cameo? Why only that and nothing else?"

Andy, despite his predicament, was as jealous as ever of Chablis. When she showed up with Sam, he had scowl on his face. Chablis introduced him, but Andy was cold toward Sam, even when Chablis said he was there to help. Cleaned up, Sam was a pretty good looking man, better looking than Andy, in fact. Then again, Andy had never cut a very dashing figure, even when he was young.

Sam said, "The cameo was penned on her right chest?"

Andy, still not happy with Sam's presence, muttered, "Yeah."

Sam rubbed his chin and said, "That was my last gift to her. I had another one that night for her but never got to give it to her, a silver chain. Actually, she liked that cameo. She always said that I finally did something right. Yeah, maybe I did, but it didn't keep her. She still dumped me."

Andy, now beginning to thoroughly resent Chablis bringing Sam, looked directly at her and said, "So what can this loser you brought along do for me? His wife used to call him a low life begging wimp bum."

Sam smiled and said, "Buddy, I may be a loser and a low-life wimp bum, but I am out here and you are in there. I had rather be me than you."

Chablis interjected, "I don't need you two duelling. Andy, he is here to help and so am I. I suggest you be a little more courteous."

Andy hung his head down and Sam looked at Chablis and smiled. Chablis said to Sam, "So, you only saw those two people from the back that entered the building while you were outside. You think you could recognize them?"

"Sure I could, no doubt about it. One was short and chubby. The other was tall and thin. The thin guy was partially bald. The short one had white flecks on the back of his hair."

Chablis looked at Andy and said as she was getting up, "Hang in there. You will be out soon. I promise."

As she was leaving Andy, almost crying, shouted, "I love you."

Chablis said to herself, "just words, anybody can say them whether they mean them or not." Anyway, she did not want to burden Andy with any more problems at the present, so not meaning it, because it had been destroyed by Andy, she replied, "I love you, too."

As they walked out of the holding area, Sam looked at her and said, "You don't sound very convincing when you say that."

Chablis turned toward Sam, looked up at him as they were walking and said, "They are just words, Sam. You should know that as well as I do. I am sure Mai-Mai must have said that to you a few times. He has enough problems to deal with. There is no need for me to put another burden on him right now."

Sam grinned and said, "You are a kind person Chablis. Most women whose husband did what he did would simply say to hell with him."

Chablis, almost laughing, replied, "Yeah, just call me St. Chablis."

CHAPTER 9
SHE HAD HIM INSIDE HER

Sam and Chablis went back to her apartment and Chablis pulled out all the things she had collected connected to the case and spread them on the kitchen table – the newspaper headlines, the address book and other paraphernalia that might have some relevance. Sam looked though the address book, scanning the names. Chablis could see it was causing him pain, so she reached over to take it from him. He looked up at her and said, "It's OK. She is gone and what she was is gone with her. I am not going to let her take me with her. When you offered me a hand up, I decided right then that there was at least one person left who cared about me. You were laughing when you called yourself St. Chablis, but I am not laughing. To me, you are a saint."

Chablis smiled and Sam got a concerned look on his face as he bored in on something in the address book. Chablis instinctively said, "What is it?"

He shoved the book across to her with a look of accomplishment on his face and said, "Check it out under Z." Hand written were the words, *Know about him, see M.R. at R.*

Chablis immediately went to the M's and there it was M.R., Marcus Ruffalo. She sighed and said, "It means Marcus Ruffalo and the R is the

Rathskeller Club. The other we will have to work on."

Sam smiled and said, "Want to go out with a reformed drunk tonight to the Rathskeller Club?

Chablis gave him a wink and said, "I'll get dolled up. You can use the hall bathroom. I have an en-suite. Check in the closet. You are Andy's size. Wear whatever you want."

The Rathskeller was in uptown Manhattan and the club attracted what would be termed the trendy crowd – those people who like to be seen as they arrogantly show off their affluence in all their fine clothes and opulent jewellery most of which they buy on instalment, because no matter how much they make it is not enough to fund their extravagant lifestyle.

The opulent dining and showroom, with giant oak columns that featured pairs of angels holding bells and gold-leaf ceilings with magnificent chandeliers sparkling overhead, complimented the vintage entertainment from big bands and a piano player who delicately played old waltzes that had long ago been forgotten by the modern set, but were now being brought back by a man who obviously appreciated quality. He had made the place opulent with a lure of the lavish. In descriptive terms the place was shaken, not stirred. It was definitely a place to be seen in all your glamour. Yet, Chablis in her $12 blouse, $14 skirt, $4 belt and $18 high heels was the classiest woman in the place. She knew how to make cheap look chic.

Chablis actually felt good walking in with Sam. He cleaned up very nicely she thought, and was a genuinely nice guy who just had the misfortune to love the wrong woman. As usual, when Chablis walked in with her smooth gliding stride that accentuated the sway of her hips, men's heads were turned and women began to feel uncomfortable with the competition for attention. The irony was that Chablis bought her clothes at Wal-Mart, as she did her jewellery, and she didn't really care whether the men looked or not. Ok, actually she did enjoy it.

They sauntered over to the bar and took a seat. The tall, lean bartender who wore thick, horn-rimmed glasses looked at them and said, "What may I get you two to drink?" Chablis, a non-drinker asked for a coke. Sam, with a bit of a grimace said, "OK, two cokes."

Chablis looked at him and smiled. "Sam, I am neither a nurse maid nor a reformer. You have a right to drink if you want."

Sam, showing a modicum of pride in himself, said, "I'll stick it out as long as I can, but I am not promising anything."

When the bartender sat the drinks down, Chablis asked, "Mr. Ruffalo around tonight?"

The bar tender nodded toward an ornate staircase that swirled down from overhead to their far left. Coming down the staircase was a portly man. The bartender said, "That is Mr. Ruffalo."

Ruffalo got to the bottom of the stairs, turned to his left and walked with his back to Chablis and Sam. Sam, almost whispering, said as he looked at the flecks of white hair on the back of his head, "That is the guy I saw go into Mai-Mai's."

"Interesting, now we have to figure out how to find out if he has the cameo. If he does, we have our killer," said a pensive Chablis.

"So, do we just approach him and ask?"

Chablis, coyly replied, "No, what we do is get on the inside and see if we can't get the low down on just what this guy might be up to."

Sam looked puzzled. "What do you mean get on the inside?"

"I mean I am going to vamp this guy Sam. I am going to make a play for him. Make him think I am interested and get into his psyche, work his mind and use my body to find that broach. We produce the cameo and we produce the killer."

Sam, a bit shocked at her brazenness, said, "You going to sleep with the guy to get to the truth?"

"Sam, I have slept with hundreds of guys. It's only sex; don't make it a big deal. Sex is just a recreational activity. It rarely has anything to do with love. People like to think it does, but the reality is much deeper than that. You use what you have to get at the truth, because as that old saying goes the truth will set you free. Only in this case, the truth will set Andy free."

Sam, already in awe of Chablis begin to stutter, "But, but, I, I mean you are so nice."

Chablis chuckled. "Sam, nice girls have sex, too."

Sam, sighing and taking in a deep breath, said, "It's just that I hate to see you have to do that. Isn't there another way?"

Chablis, with her right hand, pushed the cascading hair on her right side back behind her shoulder. "OK, Sam. Let's do this. Let's see if we can get jobs here. Let's get on the inside and maybe we can learn something that will give us a clue where the broach might be."

Chablis motioned to the bartender to come over and said to him, "So, who do we see and where do we see them to get a job here."

The bartender, seeming delighted at the thought of Chablis being around, was eager to provide the information. "Mr. Ruffalo himself does all the hiring. Come in around 10 on Wednesday. That is when he auditions talent for the floor show and also hires any waitresses or staff. You he'd hire on the spot as a waitress. Believe me, just come in and you got the job, even if he doesn't need you, I can assure you that there will be a job offer. Mister, I am afraid you don't have the kind of equipment that will guarantee you a job."

Chablis, knowing a secret neither man was privy to, said to the bartender, "If only you knew."

The bartender, unaware of what Chablis was referring to, with a quizzical look on his face said, "What you mean lady?"

Chablis, enjoying the secret she was keeping, replied, "As I said, if you only knew."

The bartender let it go, figuring it was her private joke. He looked at Sam and said, "Too bad you aren't a piano player." Then pointed at the piano player, and continued, "That dude over there leaves tomorrow. He is moving to New Hampshire. Retiring, after tinkling the ivories for 40 years."

Chablis and Sam looked at each other and laughed. Yeah, Sam had an in to the job, and

Chablis would definitely get a job as a waitress. After all, who wouldn't hire Chablis to work in a fancy, lavish, swank grandiose place like the Rathskeller, where opulence and beauty went hand-in-hand?

The next day at 9:30 AM, Chablis and Sam entered the club dressed for action. Well, at least Chablis was dressed for action.. In fact, she was dressed to kill. She was a weapon of alluring destruction that lay waste to all before her on the battlefield of sexuality. Her alluring nature flirted with all. She was the wine none could decline. Each man who gazed upon her felt a surge of excitement in that erogenous zone that rules their minds. Each wanted her by his side. Yet, one could sense that the love of this woman could not be corralled. It could not be confined. Above the highway sign that directs one to the freeway of unbridled passion was a bold warning: *proceed at your own risk*!

Yes, this was a woman who was dynamite with a sizzling fuse that titillated desire as it flashed along to its ultimate climax. This was an explosion waiting to happen.

Yet, all the innate sexuality of the woman could not betray her true beauty which lay beneath in the sweetness of a heart that beat with the rhythm of kindness, generosity and compassion. Her bronzed skin, her cascading black hair, her deep-set dark eyes that danced with erotic intensity and those tantalizingly luscious, moist, succulent, thick, pouty lips gave her a smile as warm as a winter fire that would fill the Pope with desire.

When she looked at you, she seemed to be staring into your soul saying "fire your cupid's arrow and when it pierces my heart I will pour out, not blood, but the Bacchanalian wine of debauchery that will put you in rapturous contentment."

The provocative sway of her hips seemed to be playing a melody of love that pleaded for you to take her home with you that night and play games of sweet love until dawn with her in your arms.

If there is a God who makes us all, on Chablis, he worked overtime. If he is an artist, then Chablis was his masterpiece. She was his Sistine Chapel, his Mona Lisa. This was his greatest work of art. Streaking sunsets are beautiful, painted rainbows brighten the sky, rolling hillsides are serene, splashing flowers illuminate the soul, shading white clouds floating high in the sky offer tranquility, but of all the wonders made, there is none that is as fair as the smile he painted on Chablis' face.

Ruffalo was a man with an air of authority. He seemed to relish how people bowed in fear before him and how they acquiesced to his perceived superiority. His was a manifestation of what motivates so many people to lord their exaltedness over others. He enjoyed making people cower before him. He was a small man with a big ego. That ego was simply a cover for what deep inside was an inferiority complex. Like so many people with big egos, underneath he was just a scared little man who used intimidation to mask his inferiority of mind, body and soul.

Like a great ruler of all that he surveyed, as Ruffalo was descending his stairwell from what he, no doubt, considered the thrown room of his empire, Chablis and Sam were messing around with the piano in the main dining room. Sam handed Chablis some sheet music he always carried in his suit pocket and began playing his version of *The Great Pretender*, which he had rewritten to reflect his feelings about Mai-Mai back when she first left him. Chablis, who always loved to sing, used the folded copy Sam handed her and was belting out the song like a torch singer in a blues club.

I remember an old song my mother listened to.
She even sang along
as she moved about the house.
I now am sadly humming it myself,
Because within me there is a fire I cannot douse.

Oh yes I am the great pretender.
Pretending I am doing well.

Chablis: Avenging Angel for the Forgotten
In the City of Lost Hope

My need is such I pretend too much.
I am so lonely but few can tell.
Oh yes, I am the great pretender.
Adrift in a world of my own.
I play the game but to my shame.
You've left me to dream all alone.

You are with another and you do not pretend.
You are gay and carefree like a clown.
While I am nursing a broken heart,
Because you are no longer around.

In my heart there is something I cannot conceal.
My spirit is in shambles, broken and torn.
I sometimes pretend that you are still around.
But I just get more forlorn.

My mother sang it so well long ago.
Now, all I can do is wear a frown.
Yes I am the great pretender.
Pretending you are still around.

Immediately fascinated by the singing and piano playing, Ruffalo, glanced over at Chablis and was mystified by the husky, soft, melodic voice coming from such a demure, dainty, magnificent creature that graced his club. He had never laid eyes on such an alluring woman, and with his money, prestige and power, he had more women fawning over him than the Boston Marathon had runners on race day. He simply was mesmerized by Chablis' incredible beauty and sexual allure as he turned toward the elevated stage and made his way over to Sam and Chablis so that he might get a closer look at was a delight to the ears, but also a delight to the eyes. He stood and stared as she continued to sing.

Upon a few people in this world great blessings of beauty, poise, elegance and gracefulness are bestowed. Chablis was one of those people, and the instant he sat down at the table in front of the stage area, Marcus Ruffalo was enamoured with her. When Chablis and Sam momentarily stopped their playing and singing, Ruffalo pleaded "no, no, please go on, please go on."

As they continued their performance, Ruffalo could not take his eyes off Chablis. He looked upon her as a Goddess and her smile made his heart palpitate with desire. He thought that if her smile could be held before dying people, it would lift their spirits and give them hope. That smile could melt the cruellest of hearts with its radiance, even in a man like Marcus Ruffalo. He could not take his eyes off those thick, luscious, ruby lips that offered untold delights to anyone lucky enough to taste the nectar of ecstasy that flowed from them. Ruffalo was in lustful frenzy.

Chablis could see in Ruffalo's eyes the effect she was having on him. Nothing in heaven or earth has yet been availed to extirpate a prejudice rooted in men for that which offers a glorious romp in paradise with a lustful woman. Ruffalo's mind was headed into the titillating ground of debauchery where men's aspirations always seem to point. His desires sought the purest joy in Chablis' arms. He saw her as eyes to the blind; feet to the lame, manna to the hungry. He had to have her.

As she finished up her song, he applauded and said, "Hired, both of you. You can start tonight. What are your names?"

A bit shocked by the offer, Chablis said, "Hired as what?"

Ruffalo replied, "What else, as a singer and a piano player. You two are an absolute natural for this place. People love a good torch song. Not everybody goes for the modern junk that passes as music. I want you to sing the old standards. This place needs that. Hell, I need that. It makes me feel good. What do you say? I'll give you $2000 a week and all the food you want. Take your meals here."

Chablis and Sam looked at one another and laughed as Chablis said, "I am a waitress, and Sam here was planning on bussing tables."

"OK, hired for that then, but you aren't going to make 2 grand a week doing that. Come on, make me happy and sing another melody for me. What you say? Come on, one more song. How about

another love song, something sad? I like sad love
songs."

Sam reached in his pocket. Pulled out a folded 8
½ X 11 piece of paper and handed it to Chablis.
"Think you can sing that? It's another one I
rewrote when she left me."

Chablis took it from Sam, and said, "OK."

The melody was haunting and the words cut
right through to the heart with Chablis' soft
melodic voice straining with so much emotion that
it brought Ruffalo to the edge of his seat.

In my pain, I am reminded of
what I have done wrong.
And suddenly, I think of
the George Jones song

He said I'll love you 'til I die
She told him you'll forget in time
As the years went slowly by
She still preyed upon his mind.

Those lines remind me of our commitment
To one another to endure through better or worse.
Yet, it is I who has all the pain.
And now she thinks me insane.

He kept her picture on his wall
Went half crazy now and then

Chablis: Avenging Angel for the Forgotten
In the City of Lost Hope

He still loved her through it all
Hoping she'd come back again.

Those lines bring sadness to the mind.
Making it impossible to survive
In a crazy state of pain,
Knowing her heart I might not gain.

He kept some letters by his bed
All dated 1994
He had underlined in red
Every single I love you.

My life began in 1994
Because I had her to adore,
But then she walked away.
Oh, if only she would stay.

I went to see him just today
Oh, but I didn't see no tears
All dressed up to go away
First time I'd seen him smile in years.

Those lines remind me that my smile is gone.
The tears spill like falling rain.
There is nowhere for me to go.
My spirits are so low.

He stopped loving her today
They placed a wreath upon his door
And soon they'll carry him away
He stopped loving her today.

J. Wayne Frye   223

Again, Ruffalo stood and applauded as did all the others there. He shouted, "Damn great writing, changing an old standard into a modern version that touches the heart, great piano playing – just great. You really know how to tickle the ivories. And the singing ma'am, the singing is like a nightingale. I want you two playing together tonight. Come-on what name do I put on the marquee?"

Chablis wanted to use fake names for fear of recognition. She could get fake social security cards from a friend, so she said, "Chandra Gomez," and realizing that Sam's name might be connected to Mai-Mai, she decided to call him Martin Sundavol. They were in, not as a waitress and a busboy, but as entertainers.

Leaving the club, Sam said that he had no clothes nice enough to wear. Chablis looked at him and said, "Come on up to my apartment. You can wear some of Andy's clothes. You two are about the same size."

Chablis saw promise in Sam now. He had a spring to his step and that sad scowl was gone. Was this a new beginning for him? She hoped so. He was a nice guy and deserved it.

That night and the many that followed saw them become a part of the club routine and they seemed to fit in fine, but their goal was to see if Ruffalo had that cameo. They were enjoying their gig, but the purpose of being at the Rathskeller was not to see their names in lights, but to see if Ruffalo was a killer.

However, Sam did not like watching Chablis play-up to Ruffalo. It was obvious Ruffalo was enamoured with her and gradually Chablis started sitting at his private table between sets, ignoring Sam. Then, one evening Ruffalo invited her up to his office for a drink. Sam looked wearily at her as she ascended the stairs. At that moment, he realized that he was finally over Mai-Mai. Like a flash of lightning striking a tree, it hit him. He was in love with Chablis.

He seethed with anger, realizing she was up there alone with Ruffalo, but he kept his temper under control, because they were on a mission to prove a man innocent of murder. Chablis had to do what was necessary to uncover the truth. Sam strolled over, sat down at the piano and played Moonlight Sonata.

As Chablis walked into Ruffalo's office with him, he motioned for her to follow him to the painting of Dempsey vs. Firpo he had on the far wall to the right of his desk. She couldn't believe he would be so stupid. He pulled the picture from the wall, sat the painting down on the floor and there was a safe. With her standing beside him, he made no effort to shield her from seeing the combination. Even the numbers he used for the combination showed a lack of concern, 36-23-36.

He opened it and removed a small silver box. Chablis just knew she was about to get Mai-Mai's cameo as a gift. He handed the box to her and said, "A little gift of appreciation for your fine service to the club."

Chablis excitedly opened the jewellery case, but there was immediate disappointment. It was a broach alright, but not Mai-Mai's. She faked a smile and fawned over Ruffalo as if she was genuinely appreciative, but her enthusiasm was all contrived. Yet, she now had the combination to the safe, where Mai-Mai's broach might lay waiting to be discovered.

After a few pleasantries and an offer of Champaign, which the non-drinker, Chablis, turned down, she excused herself and returned to do her last set of songs by the piano. She informed Sam that she had the safe combination, but he seemed not really interested. She wondered what was bothering him.

Sam was rather pensive, but, as always; he accompanied Chablis to her apartment by bus and then a short stroll. For the first time, she asked him in.

He excitedly replied, "What?"

Chablis: Avenging Angel for the Forgotten
In the City of Lost Hope

Chablis, smiling, pointed to the all-night corner grocery and said, "It is 3:00 AM. Go get some eggs. I am all out. I'll fix us some bacon and eggs. I am inviting you up to my place, silly."

Sam felt a surge of excitement and said, "OK. I'll be right back."

Chablis, a woman of infinite wisdom, had figured out what the problem was. Sam was in love with her, and he was upset about her going up to Ruffalo's office. Well, she had feelings for him, too. She wasn't sure it was love yet, but there was an attraction. Yes, he was fighting alcoholism, but it had been four weeks since he had a drink as far as she knew. At least he had not had one in her presence, and they were together most of their waking hours. Still, she wondered what he would think when she told him the truth about herself. Would he be repulsed or would he see that her anatomy had nothing to do with her truly being a woman? Some guys could handle it, some couldn't. Well, it didn't really matter, as she had no intention of having sex with him anyway.

After finishing the bacon and eggs, Sam helped her wash the dishes. As he was putting the plates in the cabinet, he noticed on the upper shelf several bottles of whiskey. Chablis said, "For my guests, Sam. Of course, you are a guest, so if you want a drink I would not say no, because it is not my place to tell you not to drink."

Sam smiled and said, "Don't need one, thanks."

Chablis was so pleased with him. She felt a surge of excitement and was thinking, "Should I or shouldn't I? I know he wants me really bad, but he is too much of a gentleman to force the issue. Why he hasn't even kissed me yet."

They sat down in the living room; Chablis on the sofa and Sam in the overstuffed chair across from her. Chablis, knowing she had fantastic legs, could not resist crossing them, causing her extremely short skirt to expose lots of thigh, which Sam thoroughly enjoyed looking at with intensity.

Chablis, loving the game of seduction simply could not resist. Slowly, she uncrossed her legs, allowing them to began to inconspicuously creep open, allowing a sliver of a view between her slightly-parted legs. She crossed and uncrossed her legs intermittently while using what she always playfully referred to as the up-skirt tease. At one point, she shut her eyes and pretended to lull asleep for a bit, causing her legs to part more and more in a restful oblivious way. After all, it was the morning so with all of her yawns and eye-rubs, it was obvious that she was easy prey for a willing man.

She saw Sam's gaze drifting in between her legs. From what she could tell he appeared aroused and frustrated while trying to maintain a semblance of indifference, as though there wasn't a hot woman with sexy legs and an amazing view up her short skirt right in front of him. He seemed like he was trying not to look but still very compelled to do so. He crossed his legs and made what seemed like a conscious effort to look at every other part of the room except in her direction. There was absolutely no conversation. Inevitably, his focus would always come back to between her legs. OK thought Chablis, I want this man bad, but I must level with him first. "Sam, you want me don't you?"

Sam, thoroughly shocked by Chablis' brazenness, replied, "Damn, Chablis, you know I do, but I haven't been with a woman in over three years."

Smiling, Chablis replied, "It's like riding a bicycle Sam. You never forget how, but there is something I have to tell you first in order to avoid any surprises."

Sam, jokingly said, "OK, I know you can't be a man, so what is the surprise?"

Chablis let a slow smile creep across her face and said, "Well, no I am not a man, but I am a non-op transsexual."

You could see the shock on Sam's face, but it was not disdain or disapproval, just shock at the revelation that this woman had a penis rather than a vagina. He said, "You are joking?"

"No Sam, no joke. However, if you have a problem with it, I understand."

Sam contemplated for a few seconds before saying, "Well, I think you know I am in love with you Chablis. You can't choose who you love. There are certain things I could not do. That doesn't mean I am not interested."

Chablis winked at him and motioned for him to come over and sit on the sofa. He did not hesitate. When he sat beside her, they kissed passionately for what seemed like an eternity. Chablis whispered in his ear, "You are going to like it Sam. I can do more with what I have than any woman could ever do for you. When you are inside me, you will feel like you have parked your member in the parking lot of love."

She provocatively led him toward the bedroom. Chablis turned, sighed and said, "Sam, I am a transsexual, and I know what kind of man you are, so I know you don't look with disdain on me, but I also know that you are used to women who have a different anatomy than I do. You are a straight man, but you are a man with an open mind. One who is kind, caring and generous, but that does not change the fact that you have only had sex with women who have a vagina. I can't offer you that. I

J. Wayne Frye

don't want to disappoint you. I think I am falling in love you Sam McCloud, but I will give you up rather than have you disgusted with me. I am not ashamed of whom I am, but I live as a genetic woman. Most people do not even know, but when it comes time for lovemaking, that is a different story."

Sam smiled, reached out and embraced her, pulling her tightly into his warm arms that seemed to offer comfort and hope where there had been none for awhile. As the short Chablis rested her head on the left side of his chest, she could feel his heart beating rhythmically. Sam leaned down and whispered in her left ear, "Chablis, I love you, not your anatomy. I may be timid, even apprehensive, and certainly ignorant of how to make love to a woman like you, but I will learn. I will learn because I want to bring you pleasure and happiness. The past few weeks you have given me something I thought was lost when Mai-Mai left me, something that left a hole inside me, an emptiness that put me on the precipice of desperation that has sent me on the three year spiral into misery that I thought could be treated with alcohol. I had fallen into a dark pit of hopelessness until you reached down, pulled me up and made me whole again. You are the woman with whom I am going to spend the rest of my life. I will never let you go. Mai-Mai's murder was not the end for me. Now that I have you, I realize it was the beginning."

Chablis: Avenging Angel for the Forgotten
In the City of Lost Hope

Chablis wept, sobbing as she melted, not just into his arms, but into his heart. She looked up at him blissfully and said through tears of joy, "Sam, I imagine us sitting on a pier somewhere in the soft moonlight as we listen to the waves gently roll in. I am resting my head on your shoulder as you put your arm around me and pull me close. I look up at you and say, 'this is so romantic'. From that moment on, you and I will be the magic elixir of affection and devotion."

She continued to rest her head on his chest for awhile and then she sensually looked up at him. There was wantonness, lust and desire that seemed to leap from deep within her and burn itself into Sam's brain like a raging fire of carnal yearning as she whispered in her soft husky melodic voice words that few would ever think could come from a woman as demure, sweet and proper acting as Chablis. "Sam McCloud, I am about to give you the fuck of your life."

Chablis pushed Sam to the bed and made him sit down as she dropped to her knees between his legs and looked up with her sparking dark eyes and those luscious, thick lips letting a mischievous devilish smile slowly creep across them as she gently tugged at his belt, unfastening it while continuing to gaze into Sam's penetrating green eyes that were dancing with delight at the coming pleasure that was about to sweep him into paradise, corral his heart and lock it up in the ecstasy of a moment that would last a lifetime in his mind and embolden him to let all his inhibitions gently float into a harmonious sea of tranquility. This was their moment - the moment when their bodies would release the pent up emotions that had been boiling beneath the surface for so long. They would meld their bodies into one and play a melodious symphony of buoyant hope with the optimistic covenant of blissfulness that awaited them together in a future filled with hope and promise.

With his pants now around his ankles, Sam reached down and slowly and deliberately pulled Chablis from her knees. He artfully stepped out of his shoes and pants as he pulled her short dress up over her shapely hips, stopping momentarily to caress them before gliding the dress over her stomach and her outstretched arms. All the while, Chablis' heart was racing furiously as she anxiously waited to get naked and offer herself completely to Sam.

Standing naked, except for her panties, Chablis unbuttoned Sam's shirt and peeled it off, tossing it onto the floor. Then she pulled his briefs down, his giant member stiffly saluting her beauty. As Sam stepped out of his briefs, Chablis, turned toward the top of the bed, looked back over her left shoulder, reached down and grabbed his erect manhood with her left hand. She tugged on it, making Sam follow her like she was a guide leading a tour of carnal delights. Smiling, she said as she continued pulling him eagerly toward the bed, "Hey, if I run out of closet space, I have a new place to hang my clothes."

Laughing, they made their way to the bed, and she pushed Sam down without even removing the bedspread. He lay there shaking with anticipation, his stiff organ standing like a flag pole. Chablis looked at him and said, as she slowly removed her panties. "OK Sam, this is the moment of truth for you. I am about to see if you love me as much as you say you do."

Chablis' panties fell to the floor and Sam, staring at her magnificently proportioned body, said, "I see the most beautiful woman whom I have ever gazed upon."

Smiling, Chablis moved to him. She artfully and deliberately crawled between his legs and took Sam to that land that glistens in the mind - that land where peace and tranquility make you float gently on a cloud of contentment. Her warm, inviting mouth and luscious lips worked like a chamber of delight on Sam, making him breathe with a rhythmic cadence of lustfulness as he moaned with felicitous contentment. His eyes rolled back into his head and he let out a long moan as his joy juice exploded furiously into Chablis, ramming against the back of her throat and trickling down inside her, allowing her to taste the nectar of ecstasy that flowed from him. He was a part of her now. Yes, she had him inside her.

CHAPTER 10
IT WAS BROKEN AGAIN

All the anxiety Chablis carried, the frustrated dreams, the incomprehensible cruelty and fear of extinction from the interior view of the human condition had slowly eroded the hope and any perceived salvation from the life she accepted rather than the life she could have had. The bellow of her faith and doubt against darkness and the silence of the eternal search for meaning was one of the most terrible tests of abandonment and the terrified grasping of that which is illusionary, at best, made her easy prey for a man like Andy who imprisoned her in the pit of self-denial in service to a man who had pushed her into the deep abyss of containment, rather than allowing her to soar with the eagles to unimaginable heights.

Andy had been a Svengali of deception who through the most subtle means had artfully disguised his evil intentions under the "I love you" manipulation that makes women swoon and sigh as these men beg, plead, cry and cajole their way into making it impossible for women to free themselves from their grip. Everything always boils down to being justified by the term, "but I love you." I want to know where you are at all times, because "I love you." I want you to sacrifice your career while allowing mine to flourish, because "I love you." I want to keep you from even talking to other men, because they have evil intentions and I want you to abrogate your independence to protect you from them because "I love you." I want you to always be immaculately made up and ravishingly dressed, not because of my ego gratification, but so all my friends can see how lucky I am to have such an incredibly beautiful woman by my side, because "I love you." Ah, and finally, I always monitor your computer, your cell-phone and e-mail to make 100% sure that you are not falling prey to scam artists on the internet, because "I love you."

There are countless successful women, and Chablis was one of them, who abrogate their independence, because they fall prey to men whom they think love them. Love is not control. Love is not just uttering the words. Love is not making promises and then always finding an excuse to not deliver. These women may not suffer physical abuse, but they suffer a more subtle abuse that imprisons them, and they cannot even see the bars that keep them confined in a cell of manipulation that is hidden behind subtlety and clandestine insidiousness.

Even though loved ones, like Aaron Adams in Chablis' case, can see through the deceit, these otherwise smart women cannot be made to see what is happening because they are blinded by infatuational attachment. The truth is these women are involved with a sociopath or psychopath whose primary role is to suck the life out of them.

Chablis: Avenging Angel for the Forgotten
In the City of Lost Hope

Only by demeaning these women do the men make themselves feel exalted. They fear the woman's success, because her success indicates their failure. Still, each time they demean the woman they will grovel, beg and plead for forgiveness, only to repeat the same routine again and again. Of course, the justification is always that phrase, "but I love you."

Another favourite ploy of these men is to use material things to convince the women of how much they love them. They will borrow on credit cards to wine and dine these women. The true purpose, however, resides deep in the men's psyche where they see themselves as somehow exalted as a result of conquest. Then, when the bills for the dinners, the clubbing and the expensive jewellery come due, they are reduced to borrowing from Peter to pay Paul. Some men, if they feel confident enough, will even start asking for help paying the bills, but the truly wise ones avoid this tactic until far down the road when they have the woman hooked financially as well as emotionally. Fortunately, Andy had avoided doing this to Chablis, but they were always on the brink of insolvency, because of Andy's inability to refrain from over-spending.

Unlike Chablis, many women, who have led sheltered lives are extremely vulnerable to the "but I love you" syndrome, particularly ones who have an unstable family background, as they fall for the trap set by the man who uses his own family as a manipulative tool to keep the woman in her chains. The woman is made to accept the "rules" of the family which may include acceptance of homophobia, religion or lack of religion, drug use, alcohol use, moral imperatives, etc… Of course, the key is to massage the mind gradually and make the person unaware through subtlety that they are bending to amalgamations of thought that they would have never acquiesced to previously. The woman is expected to adjust her lifestyle while the man continues living his life with only modest modification to satisfy the woman whom he wants to keep under control. The man is wearing a mask of deception and using the term "but I love you" to conceal his true self that is only manifested periodically and then quickly covered up by the aforementioned begging, pleading, crying and cajoling. Chablis had constantly fallen victim to this manipulative technique used by Andy.

These patterns are primarily manifested in men with low self-esteem and with addictive personalities. These men charm a woman by putting her at the centre of their universe; making the woman feel like she never felt before. Then seemingly out of nowhere comes the anger and with it the patterns of abuse, especially manifestations and accusations of the woman's uselessness because she doesn't earn as much as the man or that her job, even if she makes more money than the man does, is somehow less important. Of course, in Chablis' case, even though Andy didn't want her to work, he was always throwing the fact she didn't back in her face.

These manipulative masters treat the woman like the only woman who ever existed. But once lulled into that false sense of believing that, the man feels free to end the honeymoon and start demeaning the woman. Of course, the demeaning episodes are always followed by repentance. This is a pattern that will continue until one day, when the man has achieved his objectives, and completely destroyed the woman's ability to think for herself, he will stand triumphant. All the while this manipulation is occurring, the woman will be unable to see what she has allowed to happen, because she is so much in love she refuses to see the patterns of abuse to which she willingly acquiesces.

If the opportunity presents itself, eventually the man will seek out other women, because this will just solidify his feeling that he is a "real man." Andy was always reminding Chablis how desirable he was to other women. These kind of men will avow fidelity, but in their hearts, they are capable of the vilest infidelities. After all, they are "real man" with a hairy chest, muscular arms and the ability to kill at will to protect their "property," because that is what the man considers the woman. He looks on a marriage licence as a deed of ownership.

Women will also cry out that these men are not smart enough to be initiating all these manifestations of control. Truthfully, some of these men might not be smart enough to even realize what they are doing, but whether they are doing these things consciously or subconsciously that does not make the results any less insidious. Andy had definitely been aware of what he was doing to control Chablis, but it was OK in his meagre mind, because he was the man, and in his way of thinking, the man was always in control.

Chablis' love for Andy had blinded her from reality? But now her eyes had been opened, and she realized no matter how much a woman thinks she loves a man, he can be replaced with something better. A woman does not have to just shrug her shoulders and say, "well, everybody has their flaws." Yes they do, but some flaws are worse than others. Chablis no longer felt compelled to accept the mediocre. No woman has to accept the kind of control Andy had exercised, and Chablis was now free of that.

When Chablis woke up next to Sam, she smiled at him as they greeted each other. Things had changed for Sam and Chablis. Love does that to people. She asked him to please not tell Andy, because she did not want to make his life in prison any more unbearable. Soft hearted and willing to do as Chablis wanted, Sam acquiesced without protest.

Chablis asked Sam to move out of his dingy hotel room and move in with her, which he willingly agreed to do. The two of them now were ready to get into Ruffalo's safe and locate the cameo. Then, Chablis would get Andy free from prison, and she would also free herself completely from Andy, submitting no more to the control of any man, not even Sam. In fact, Chablis felt truly free herself for the first time in years. Sam was not the kind of man who would expect to control her. He had a depth of character that even his descent into alcoholism could not diminish. Chablis could see in him a kindness, a deep-tooted goodness that let you know he could never harm anyone. Chablis never saw that in Andy. Why she asked herself did she marry him? She giggled to herself and thought about that monster between Andy's legs and decided she was a fool for a well-hung guy, but no more. Sam was average size, but he was not average when it came to depth of character. In that case, Sam was the "real man" not Andy.

That night, as Sam sat at the piano, he handed Chablis a song he had written just for her that day. She listened to the melody and rather than sing it, she read it to the crowd, and it was a song that touched her heart, touched everyone there that night with its intensity.

Chablis: Avenging Angel for the Forgotten
In the City of Lost Hope

Messengers of Love

My love for you now only knows humility.
I steal into the alleys of darkness
that surround me,
Longing to kiss one lock of your hair.
I cannot free myself, because I am your prisoner,
And I cannot break the chains that bind me.

I cannot love myself more than I love you.
I had died but was resurrected by you.
I had vanished from the
horizon of hope without you.
I had sacrificed my learning
at the altar without you.
Alas, I can only be a scholar
by knowing love from you.
I have lost all my strength in a torrent of passion.
The power to enable me can only come from you.

I am your Knight in shining armour.
Come by my side. I will open the gate to paradise.
Come settle with me, and we shall
Be neighbours with the stars.
You have been hiding for so long,
drifting endlessly in
Stormy seas where the beacon
Of my love could not reach you.

Still, you are connected to me as sure
As the fetus is connected
To the mother by the umbilical cord of life.

J. Wayne Frye   243

Chablis: Avenging Angel for the Forgotten
In the City of Lost Hope

Concealed, revealed into the unknown,
In the unencumbered, in the un-manifested
You must reach out to embrace
that which is within me.
You have been a wanderer in
the wildness of love lost.
For you, I will be the roaring ocean
Pounding the shore of hope.
Come merge with me
and leave the world of doubt,
Ignorance and turmoil behind
As we move toward the light of promise.
Be with me! Be with me! Be with me!
Please be with me!
I will open the gate to promise and security.

I desire you more than I long
For the nourishment of food or drink.
I thirst and hunger like a lost soul
For one nod of hope from you.
My body, my senses, my mind long for your taste.
I can sense your over-powering presence
in my rapidly beating heart.
Even if you are with another,
Thinking it is rapturous contentment,
I would wait with silent passion
For one gesture, one glance from you.

As I cry tears waiting for your acknowledgement,
I realize they are sacred raindrops from the heart.
They are not a mark of weakness, but of power.
They speak the words I cannot muster.

J. Wayne Frye

Chablis: Avenging Angel for the Forgotten
In the City of Lost Hope

They speak more eloquently than 100,000 tongues.
The tears are messengers of my love.

There was no applause after the reading of the song that was magnificently harmonized with Sam's playing of the Moonlight Sonata by Beethoven. The crowd was in awe of what they had heard. The beauty of it stunned them. The silence was a testament to the power of Sam's words that Chablis knew were written for her. She turned to Sam, and with tears on her eyes she mouthed the words, "I love you."

Chablis, in search of justice for her Andy, and Sam, reeling in pain from the turmoil of unrequited love for Mai-Mai had miraculously found each other and their lives had been transformed. Love comes along at the most unexpected times.

A person with less commitment and less depth of character would have let Andy rot in jail; but Chablis still had an obligation to him despite his infidelity. She could not abrogate her responsibility to see justice done. Andy was one of the forgotten ones in the city of lost hope which was in a state of inequality in a country that did not know the meaning of justice. Yes, Chablis was the avenging angel who fought against insurmountable odds to achieve the unachievable, to right injustice, to exterminate prejudice, to lay waste to oppression and to confront malfeasant disregard for fairness. That was the woman Sam wrote the song about.

Through tears, she lovingly leaned over and delicately kissed Sam, and as she did, she noticed Ruffalo descending the stairs from his office with none other than the infamous Armond Carlton. She kept her back turned to him and whispered to Sam, "It's Armand Carlton with Ruffalo. I have to keep my back turned so he won't recognize me and give us away. Let me know when he is gone."

Sam carefully followed with his eyes the two men as they moved toward the front entrance and left. He looked up and said, as he was playing *Rhapsody in Blue*, "They have left. Now is the time to get in that safe. I will keep an eye out for them. When Ruffalo returns, I will play *Moonlight Sonata* again. Duck out the door and go in the restroom beside his office and wait until I play *Let It Be* to come out. That will be the all clear signal."

"OK, this is it Sam. This is going to clear Andy, and it will also clear us for a life of contentment together." Chablis gave him a wink and headed up the stairs with 36-23-36 in her mind. It was more than a combination to a safe; it was a combination to freedom for Andy.

No one seemed to notice Chablis as she ascended the stairs. The assumption was she was going to the restroom, which was reserved for employees who worked on the main floor of the club. It was right beside Ruffalo's office. She walked to the restroom door, took a look around, then moved rapidly over to Ruffalo's office door and quickly went inside, gently closing the door behind her and stopped to make a 30 second phone call. It was dark, but she knew her way around enough to get to the wall where the safe was. She removed the picture and quickly dialled in the combination. It opened easily and there was a wad of $20 bills wrapped up on one side and two jewellery cases on the other. She artfully removed the jewellery cases and with great anticipation opened the first one which had a diamond ring in it. So, she knew that the other one must contain the cameo that belonged to Mai-Mai.

She had waited for this moment a long time. Now, she was almost reluctant to open it. Her trepidation was manifested in the rapid beat of her heart and beads of sweat forming on her brow.

Slowly and methodically, she opened the case. It was empty of jewellery, but there was a small folded piece of paper in the case. She unfolded it and walked over to the window where the neon light in front of the club cast enough light through for her to read what it said. *Dear Chandra. Excuse me, I mean Chablis. You are wasting your time. I don't have the broach. I was the man with the package who bumped into you when you were going into Mai-Mai's apartment. Sincerely, Marcus*

As she heard Sam playing *Moonlight Sonata*, she reached down and turned on the desk lamp. She sat down in Ruffalo's expensive leather chair and waited. She had no reason to be in a hurry to get out. He and Carlton had set her up for discovery. If he wanted, Ruffalo had her for robbery, even though she had stolen nothing. She sat and waited, shaking her head in frustration that she had been so naive. Where was Aaron Adams when you needed him? Yeah, he was in Sweden protecting a girl from an assassin, and here was Chablis, allowing herself to be set-up. What an amateur. However, she had one ace in the hole that the two men were not aware of. She wasn't as amateurish as they thought she was that night.

Ruffalo and Carlton walked in and Ruffalo switched on the overhead light as Chablis just swivelled from side to side in the chair very nonchalantly. Armand Carlton, with a sinister big grin spreading across his face just as Sam rushed through the door, said, "Gotcha bitch!"

Sam, running to her side, was surprised that Chablis had simply stayed in the office and made no attempt to get out. "What's going on darling?"

Chablis looked up at Sam, then at Armand and Ruffalo. "These two men are pretty smart. In fact, they are damn smart. They set me up. Our friend Ruffalo was the guy with the package in his arm I nearly bumped into when I went into Mai-Mai's. Armand here is obviously his friend. Why wouldn't he be his friend? Ruffalo is a crook and Armand is a crooked cop. What a perfect combination."

A look of extreme satisfaction on his face, Armand said, "Crooked or not bitch you are going down for attempted burglary. Maybe you and your husband can get adjoining cells or even be in the same one, because I don't know where they put freaks like you – in men's prisons or women's prisons."

Chablis said absolutely nothing, because she knew something they didn't. She sat back and let them do the talking. Sam was flabbergasted as to why she was not being more forceful. It wasn't like Chablis.

Sinisterly moving a few steps toward Chablis, Ruffalo said, "People don't mess with me Chandra or Chablis, whatever name you prefer. I just wanted to give you enough rope to hang yourself. Looks like you have done it. Armand here may even be able to tie your boyfriend into this affair as an accessory. We have you wrapped up in a nice little package. You made it so easy. Why do you think I let you see the combination? Armand said he needed you out of circulation. So, I arranged it, as a favour to him, because he has done me many favours over the years. So Chablis, you been had, babe. This should just about do it I think. You'll look good in a jail jumpsuit"

Sam reached down and took Chablis, who seemed basically unconcerned about what was happening, by the hand. He pulled her up quickly but gently from the chair and as he did, Armand pulled out his revolver, gave them a stare of intense hate and said, "You ain't going nowhere, bitch. Sit your ass down.

Chablis winked at Sam. "Don't worry Sam, Armand here is about to get a surprise. He thinks he has me all wrapped up, but I am not as dumb as he thinks."

Armand, his chest puffed out, said, "You are dumber bitch."

Chablis let that gorgeous smile spread across her lips as a man walked in behind Ruffalo and Carlton. Chablis turned to Sam and said, "Sam, meet my friend John Havoc, who just happens to be a police detective."

Carlton and Ruffalo quickly turned and there stood John Havoc like a stone wall of contempt. He said, "Nice to meet you Sam. It appears you two are not too particular with whom you hang out."

Armand shouted, "What the fuck you doing here you internal affairs pig? I got this bitch dead to rights, maybe him too."

John shook his head vigorously. "You don't have shit Armand. Chablis called me from this office before she opened the safe, said she had a suspicion that there was a broach in the safe that would prove her husband innocent of Mai-Mai McCloud's murder and that she was afraid if she didn't get it right away that Ruffalo might get rid of it. I told her under my authority to check it, and I would take the heat for any consequences because there is probable cause."

Chablis walked up to Ruffalo with Sam by her side, looked over at John and said, "Unfortunately there is no broach. Guess the guy is innocent after all."

Ruffalo said, "I was in the apartment and she was already dead when I got there. That is why I was getting out of there. The package I had was a gift for Mai-Mai."

Havoc said as he looked over at Armand, "And you knew this didn't you? That, my friend, is suppressing evidence. I suggest you get yourself an attorney, because there will be an internal affairs investigation. Unfortunately Chablis, it will probably not be enough for a judge to order a new trial for Andy."

Chablis, a look of satisfaction on her face, said, "OK Johnny, but at least I brought down this bastard."

She walked right up to Armand Carlton and looked him directly in the eyes, "Who got who asshole."

He started to swing at her, but Chablis ducked under his fist and kneed him in the groin. He crumbled to the floor and Chablis looked over at John and said, "When the bastard finds his balls, tell him Chablis Louise Chavez said, "Good night."

John gave her a smile and said, "Stay in touch Chablis."

She and Sam exited the office, went down the stairs and out the front door. The night air felt good. Hey, Chablis and Sam felt good, even though there was not a broach in the safe. Bringing arrogant jerks down always feels good, and Chablis felt like an avenging angel for the many forgotten people who had suffered at the hands of Armand Carlton. She would sleep well that night, and she would do it in the arms of the new man in her life, a man whom she adored.

As they strolled the streets of Manhattan together, all the extemporaneous noise, the hustle and bustle of Friday night when people are celebrating the end of the week's slavery to the corporations that keep them in bondage as workers and consumers seemed superfluous to the joy they were sharing just being with each other.

It is said that life is nothing but a journey to death, but these two lovers were now on the journey together, arm-in-arm, moving ever forward to meet a new day of challenges secure in the knowledge of their love. Life was a maze of circumstances, but together they would meet them with vigour. They would plough their field of hope and promise, and the crop harvested would sustain them with the assurance that they would be there for each other. Weeds might try to sully the crop, but they would be well-armed against any folly. They would laugh in the face of adversity and not allow any vindictive tripe to mar their lives.

If there is a heaven, Sam and Chablis were in it. Heaven was made by them that night, but not by any God. The strong connection made them feel whole. They were not a tiny plant in the shade of a giant oak. They were the oak that night. They were mighty champions bold and free of any restraint.

These two were strolling deities perfected and emboldened with assurance. The measured way they walked, the countenance on their faces, their shoulders reared back and chests stuck out belied two people who had found the yellow brick road to happiness. They would not allow a chirping sparrow to fall, a mockingbird to whimper, a humming bird to have its flutter stayed or an eagle to be denied its glorious freedom to sail the heavens above.

Hope springs eternal in the human breast, and these two people who had lost hope found it again in each others arms that faithful night. The human soul is uneasy and confined but it expatiates in a life to come. Well, that life had come to Sam and Chablis. Now, these two from devotion would never stray. Theirs was a solar walk among the stars, a stroll through the Milky Way. Behind a clear topped mountain of hope, they embraced a world of possibilities on a happy island free of torment.

Chablis was an angel in his arms, her wings of kindness fluttering to put out any serpent's fire, as her faithful Sam accompanied her on journey to slay the unjust. Yes, she was an angel, but to Sam she was his God. He worshipped her as her heavenly body shined with the light of promise, hope, aspiration and expectation. Chablis, to Sam, was a sun-kissed nectar-laden flower in the full-bloom of spring, a balmy morning dew, a mine of a thousand treasures and a canopy to keep the rain of sorrow from touching him as it once did. She was the perfection of his life, the eternal spring that promised a cloudless sky for eternity.

J. Wayne Frye

That first night of blissful love-making, Sam was a bit squeamish in regards to Chablis' anatomy. Although he accepted her as a complete woman, he had been careful to avoid any direct contact with that part of her anatomy that was different from that which he had ordinarily been accustomed to when sleeping with a woman. Chablis had dealt with that most of her life, as she was attracted to straight men and her sexual enjoyment was not predicated on having that part of her anatomy included in the play during the sexual trysts she enjoyed with men. Her organisms were intense and came with regularity during anal intercourse, but she and Sam had not had intercourse that first night as she concentrated on oral stimulation and he only playfully fondled her body and delicately enjoyed savouring her perky nipples with his warm mouth and tongue. She had explained to Sam that she did not expect him to do anything for which he had an aversion. To Chablis, sex with Sam was not for recreation, but an extension of their newfound love for one another. She wanted everything to reflect that love, including the boundaries that Sam might want to observe. Anyway, Chablis had made it plain that as far as sex was concerned she could take it or leave it. She had much rather take it, because it was fun, but it was not the core of her life, nor the core of a relationship.

That night, after the frustration of not finding the cameo, she rested in Sam's arms, her naked body warm and inviting as she lay on her left side with her face buried in his chest and her right arm wrapped around his waist. The feel of her unusual female anatomy brushing against his leg did not bother Sam as he felt its slow but steady erection forming. It was something he would get used to; because this was more woman than he had ever encountered, and in his younger days, he had been quiet the dandy with the ladies.

In almost a whisper, Chablis said, "Sam, we will have to start anew on our quest tomorrow for the cameo, but tonight we shall put aside the concern over finding that cameo as we enjoy the blissfulness of deep sexual satisfaction. I am going to make you feel even better tonight than I made you feel last night. Get ready for what will replace last night's episodic exploration of sensuality with one that is going to blow your mind. I may have to call the paramedics to revive you after I am through making love to you tonight."

Sam, laughing, said sardonically, "What are you waiting for girl? I think you may be all talk and no action."

Chablis rolled over and exposed her magnificent shaped posterior for his total viewing pleasure. She rubbed it against his leg and Sam turned to his side, sliding his stiff member between her glorious cheeks and rubbing back and forth as she squeezed with precision to trap his member between the warmth of her perfectly formed cheeks. Chablis wanted it bad! He began to lick and kiss her shoulders as she continued to wiggle and squirm. She let go of his member and said "I want you to kiss my ass Sam. Go ahead big boy, kiss it." Then, she twitched and throbbed as he gently bit and kissed those curvaceous cheeks. He licked down the back of her legs, lingering on the soles of her feet, blowing on them, kissing them, and then she turned completely over flat on her stomach and jutted her posterior into the air by pulling her legs up slightly so she was resting on her knees. With it now high in the air for Sam to gaze upon with delight, she spread her legs making a provocative V shape so he could make no mistake what she was wanting.

She reached over to her nightstand and pulled out the drawer, skilfully removing the KY jelly, managing to open it with one hand. She squeezed it out, reached around and spread it where paradise awaited Sam. She whispered, "Ease into me Sam and get ready for the ride of your life."

At first Sam was actually too gentle, and Chablis said, "No baby, not that gentle. It won't break if you do it harder."

With a mighty shove he was deep inside her! He began to knead her cheeks pulling them further apart so he could get in deeper and deeper. Suddenly the pounding was so hard that slapping sounds met each thrust as Chablis encouraged him by shouting, "harder baby, harder."

He reached his hands around her stomach and hoisted her up like she was weightless, never interrupting his pounding rhythm. Chablis felt so light she found it effortless to ram backwards to meet every thrust, and she began to squeeze her sphincter muscle on his member driving him into a fury of passion. She artfully pushed him backward and coaxed him onto his back without allowing his member to slip out. She sat on him with her back facing him, riding his member, letting him see it move in and out of her. Sam began to thrust upward rapidly. He put his hands on each of her hips and began to lift her up and down on his magnificent instrument of pleasure. Sam's whole body trembled and tingled while he was inside her.

Chablis could feel when he was about ready to explode, and she would slow down gradually, whispering "Not yet baby. Not yet. I am going to make you beg for release"

Chablis loved the control she could exercise over men with her body. It gave her a sense of immense power. Then as she rode him furiously she shouted "Give it to me baby. Gush it out like a volcano blowing off the top of a mountain. Come on, I want to feel it pound my insides. I want it to rock my world, blow a hole in my soul. I want a flood of your joy juice. Flood my ass baby, flood it."

Sam plunged into her faster and harder and began letting out moans as his breathing quickened and became laboured. He suddenly went into a frenzy and thrashed so deep and hard he felt like he was tearing Chablis' insides out, but all she could do was shout, "Come on baby, come on, flood me, flood me."

With a deep sigh and a shout of "Oh, oh, oh" Sam exploded wads of hot thick liquid deep into Chablis until it flooded and oozed out and ran down Sam's member and felt warm and comforting on him. Chablis let out a satisfied moan and felt convulsions that signified she had joined Sam in the paradise of pleasure and satisfaction.

Thick pearly white droplets oozed out of Chablis and down Sam's shaft. And that was only the beginning. Chablis crawled off him, turned around and lay on top of him passionately kissing him with those luscious, thick ruby lips and then she slowly worked her way down to use those gorgeous lips and warm mouth on his member to get it ready for another frantic session of pounding. This frenzied lovemaking went on into the wee hours of the morning until Sam finally begged her, "Chablis, I can't take it anymore. I am going to die."

Chablis smiling, lovingly cradled herself in Sam's warm arms and said, "Get used to it baby. This is going to happen every night." He moaned and she laughed as they drifted off into slumber exhausted, satiated and, of course, completely satisfied.

That morning, after Chablis took another pounding from Sam, as she prepared breakfast, Sam lay in bed thinking how he wanted every moment with her to be perfect. Each day would be spent in joyous thoughts of Chablis and how he wanted to spend the rest of his life in heavenly bliss with her by his side as they floated on a cloud of love sailing high above all strife and pain. To Sam, Chablis was the ripe nectar in the flower of love that spreads out its welcoming blossoms to greet each day. With her, he had everything in life he desired. Without her, his life had been a lonely, desolate, barren desert of misery where he was dying of thirst in search of love. Chablis had quenched his thirst for affection as he saw her love spread out its warm arms and embrace him. Chablis was the blood of love that pumped through his veins, making it possible for him to live again. His heart beat with a steady rhythm of adoration for she who had become his whole word.

Connections, thought Sam, are made with the heart, not with words. He and Chablis had found each other with their hearts. Chablis was the calm that quieted his angst and worry, and she was the last chapter in his book of love. Only death could keep her from him, and even the grim reaper would find Sam a worthy opponent as he would fight to never leave her side, even when death called, because heaven would not be heaven without Chablis.

Sam turned to his right and looked out the window. The sky was turning grey. There was a storm coming. He felt a dread slowly descend upon him. Why? Why, he thought. Everything was so perfect. But the room began to swirl and his head started to pound. He felt perspiration form on his brow and his body seemed feverish. He was suddenly afraid, but afraid of what?

His descent into alcoholism was a desperate attempt to escape from the torturous memories of Mai-Mai, but those memories were gone. Yet, for some reason, at that moment in time, Sam felt a sense of insurmountable horror and a dread of some impending doom. He felt an atmosphere of sorrow. He suddenly thought what if everything between he and Chablis was a dream? What if all the laughter was really just tears in disguise?

The coming storm blackens the sky of the mind.
It threatens sanity, lucidity and happiness
Like a black shroud of doom, covering every thing.
It is as if there is something lurking within,
Waiting to destroy all hopes and dreams,

Chablis: Avenging Angel for the Forgotten
In the City of Lost Hope

Sweeping them up in the torrents
Of whirling winds that blow with
A clammy coldness warning of a coming calamity.
Contentment is shattered by fear of that
Which lurks in dark corners and awaits
In the murkiness of an unsure irresolute mind.
Hope darkens and the ill wind of despair blows
With fear, making one tremble with trepidation.

Sam's moroseness was interrupted by a naked Chablis standing in the doorway saying, "Want some more of this gorgeous body, or you want to eat breakfast. They are both available."

Sam, hiding his consternation over the feelings he was experiencing, said, "Chablis, I am exhausted. Any more sex this morning and you can call the undertaker."

Chablis grinned, winked at him and said, "Come on in the kitchen party-popper. I'm buying you some vitamins today."

All through breakfast and getting dressed, Sam tried to hide his moroseness, but the feeling of impending doom was simply overwhelming him. Silly, he thought, what do I have to be morose about? I have Chablis. I have the angel of light in my grasp. She has lifted me from the dark pit of despair into the bright sunshine of hope. He shrugged it off and asked what their next move was in pursuit of justice for Andy.

Chablis: Avenging Angel for the Forgotten
In the City of Lost Hope

Chablis, eyes sparkling with mischievous intent, said, "Miscreants be aware, the dynamic duo is about to ascend carrying the mighty sword of justice, slaying all who stand between them and the truth. But truthfully Sam, I don't know. There are suspects galore; so many people disliked Mai-Mai, but to kill her I don't really see anyone as the prime suspect. I simply don't know. I have had many cases over the years, but this one is maybe just too personal. We wasted weeks with Ruffalo, only to come to a dead end. Meanwhile, Andy languishes in prison."

Sam, that feeling of moroseness creeping slowly back over him said, "Chablis, we have to talk."

Chablis, with a questioning countenance, replied, "But we are talking."

Sam said, "Chablis, you have fulfilled your obligation to Andy. No other woman would have been as loyal as you have been. You can only do so much."

Chablis bowed her head and seemed to be talking to the floor. "He is going to rot in prison Sam for a crime he didn't commit. I know the prisons of this uncaring, vengeful nation are filled with innocent people who dared to question authority or happened to be too poor to afford a competent attorney, and I pine for their unjustified incarceration just as much as Sam's. I know I can't right all the wrongs committed against the vulnerable by an unjust society, but I was married to Andy, and I did love him at one time. I owe him nothing, I know, because of his betrayal, but I must do this for myself, if not for him. It is who I am Sam. You have to understand."

"Chablis, you have done all you can. So have I. You know, you fell for Sam's manipulations for years. Maybe darling, just maybe he is not innocent. Give it a little consideration. You have to entertain that thought."

Chablis raised her head and looked directly into Sam's eyes. "You may be right, but until that infernal cameo is found I cannot rest."

Sam, with the feeling of doom still overwhelming him said, "Don't you see Chablis. Sam had the broach. Sam tossed it away, probably threw it into the East River. You think he is dumb, but he puts up an act that you, for some reason, can't see through. He is still manipulating you. You have to face it darling. Andy killed her. They were two of a kind. They were both manipulating users who only saw people as pawns to sacrifice for their own good, so that in the end they could shout 'checkmate.' They were and are no good, pure and simple."

"Sam, I can't go on not knowing. I have to find the truth."

Chablis: Avenging Angel for the Forgotten
In the City of Lost Hope

Sighing, Sam said, "Chablis I thought my life was completely over until I met you. I was just waiting for death to claim me and ease the pain I was in, but you came into my life. I thought that I could not survive without Mai-Mai, but you lifted me up, you showed me the kindness of a real woman, not a superficial excuse of one like Mai-Mai was."

Chablis, seemingly in deep thought, replied, "I am a real woman Sam. Too many people don't understand that because they are not able to see beyond the physical. They are just ignorant people who cannot comprehend the pain and agony women like me suffer. I hide my emotions well, but I am as vulnerable as anyone else. I have struggled against bigotry all my life, and never seemed to waver, but inside I was in turmoil. Andy is a homophobic, narrow-minded bigot, but he wanted me with all my anatomical imperfections as a woman. I was so faltered that his type of man would be attracted to me. I know now that he is a manipulative bastard who used me for his own self-aggrandizement, making himself feel better because he had captured the heart of what he considered a beautiful woman. Yet, it made me feel so good to know that this type of man wanted me. I know you want me, but you are not like Andy. You are a man of substance and intelligence. You see things as they should be, not as they are. I love you, and I no longer love Andy, but I cannot forget how good and accepted he made me feel for a little while. I know it was all show and no substance now, but for awhile I felt like I had become like any other normal woman. Inside Sam, that is all I ever wanted, just to be accepted like any other woman would be."

Sam bent over and placed his hands on Chablis knees and whispered. "I knew from that first day in my dingy hotel room that you were the woman I had always really wanted. I was dead Chablis and you resurrected me. Looking into your peaceful eyes gave me a warm glow inside. I did not think I had a chance with you, but you embraced me with all my faults and gave me hope."

"Chablis stood up and said with determination, "I have to see it through Sam. I can't stop now. I can't."

Sam, now the feeling of doom completely overwhelming him, said, "Damn you Chablis. Goddamn you. You have a man who loves you, and you are throwing that away for a goddamn asshole who cheated on you, and was going to dump you anyway. Go ahead, keep chasing windmills."

Sam stormed out of the kitchen, went into the bedroom and started throwing his clothes in a suitcase. Chablis came and stood at the door, saying nothing, just watching another man she loved leave her. Was she doomed to always be alone? Was this just another chapter in a long book of broken hope?

Tears welled up in Chablis eyes and they began to cascade down her cheeks. Tough, resilient, tough-as-nails Chablis Louise Chavez was reduced to tears. Why could she not just let Andy rot, like he was going to let her rot in solitude as he ran away with Mai-Mai? Why was she incapable of ignoring the plight of anyone who suffered injustice? Why could she not just let things go? Why did she refuse to allow any room for the acceptance of that which was unchangeable? Why was it impossible for her to bend when the winds of adversity blew into life and wrecked havoc? She was a woman possessed with the pursuit of truth and justice.

His suitcase packed, Sam moved to the door where Chablis stoically stood, still saying nothing. He brushed past her and left. As the apartment door slammed, Chablis felt emptiness; it was slamming her heart too. It was broken again.

CHAPTER 11
THE CONSCIOUS WOULD OVERRULE
THE SUBCONSCIOUS

The head sometimes rules the heart.
It becomes its partner in crime.
And the person who commits the crime
Buries it in the deep recesses of the psyche,
Letting it rest there without disturbance
Unaware of the monster within.

Andy Deluca was desperately trying to contact Chablis. He managed to get her on the phone when the guard reluctantly handed him a cell phone with the admonition, "Make it quick, you got one minute. I could be seriously reprimanded for this."

Chablis picked up the phone, thinking it must be Sam calling to apologize. Surprised Andy was calling she was somewhat curt, "What you want?"

"What do I want? I just remembered something important, if you have time to listen."

Still concerned about Sam leaving, her curtness continued. "Look Andy, I am still working on things, but I am pretty busy right now. Say what you have to say and stop playing games with me."

"This isn't a game to me Chablis. It is my life. I remembered today that I saw a guy going up the stairs behind the doorman at Mai-Mai's apartment when he opened the elevator door for me. It just suddenly came to me, and I know I have seen the guy. I can't remember where, but there is something about him."

"What do you mean something about him," replied a perplexed Chablis.

"I can't figure it out, but I know who the guy was. I know I have seen him before somewhere, but I just can't put my finger on it. I just can't remember when, where or who?"

Her interest now piqued, Chablis said, "OK Andy. I have not forgotten you. You can depend on me more than you will ever know. Lie down, think long and hard, and be assured I am not deserting you. I should because you are a cheating, lying bastard, but I can't let an injustice go un-rectified, so hang in there. Chablis Louise Chavez is still on the case."

The burly prison guard motioned for Andy to hand him the phone, so he said to Chablis, "Gotta go. I will give it some thought. Don't desert me please."

Chablis, now beginning to want to prepare Andy for what was coming when he was cleared said, "Not now Andy, not now. Don't worry, not at this time."

Chablis: Avenging Angel for the Forgotten
In the City of Lost Hope

Remembering the Death of Mai-Mai

Many people turn to alcohol in times of peril. It is the drug of choice for the majority of people who flounder in the agony of self-doubt, neglect, loneliness and despair. The killer of Mai-Mai was one of those people and was actually unaware of his crime having suffered from a psychosis disorder. He had committed it yes, but within the deep recesses of his mind, he forgot how he clandestinely slipped unobserved by prying eyes into her apartment that night. He obliterated from his tortured mind the rage that made him reach down and grab the pillow from the chaise lounger and smother Mai-Mai's hideously repulsive ugliness into the oblivion of eternity. With her last breath he was free of all the offences she had perpetrated against him, but he had also freed others from the misery endured from a woman with no heart, no soul and no conscience. There were so many who breathed a sigh of relief with the news of Mai-Mai's death, all but Sam, of course, because he, at the time, did not have Chablis in his life. For him, Mai-Mai's death was just a continuation of his slide into the abyss of hopelessness where he had floundered for three years. News of her death brought a pail of even deeper misery as he realized that she would not be around to abuse him any longer. If he couldn't have Mai-Mai, he could at least have her abuse. He had bowed to it ever since she left. Oh, how he loved her.

Chablis: Avenging Angel for the Forgotten
In the City of Lost Hope

The night of the crime, as the doorman who had argued vociferously with Sam watched him quickly walk away, he turned his back when Sam got to the corner about 10 feet away. He greeted Andy, and moved toward the elevator with him, and he did not notice a solitary figure scurrying behind him and literally running up the stairs. Of course, as alluded to previously, Andy did notice the figure but just assumed it was a tenant. Exchanging pleasantries with Andy for about a minute as the elevator door was held open, gave the person on the stairs an opportunity to get to Mai-Mai's apartment. The maid had just walked out and was standing by the elevator as the figure quietly moved down the hallway without her noticing him. What luck, the door had been left unlocked by the maid who no longer wanted to endure Mai-Mai's sadistic abuse. She did not know it, but she had unlocked the door for murder.

In his pocket, the killer carried a matchbook from the Rathskeller Club where he had started to write his name on the inside cover to give to a man who was offering him a job. Then, he stopped after just writing the letter M and thought why waste my time? He stuck it in his pocket and walked away, but now he used it to place in the key pad on the door jam to keep the door from slamming shut.

Mai-Mai was standing at her desk in the living room, having just decided to write down the alias name for her husband Sam. She wanted his phone number in her book, because she always loved harassing him. She enjoyed making him crawl, beg and plead. Psychologically, she had crossed him out of her heart like so many others, so she drew a line over his name, a symbol of her disdain for him. She fingered the broach on her sweater and smiled, thinking what a fool he was to waste so much money on a woman who deplored him.

Meanwhile, the dark figure moved toward her unnoticed. She turned and immediately felt a dread as she said, "What are you doing here? What do you want?"

The man moved closer and said, "I want some peace, bitch."

As he said that, she made a dash for the bedroom, but he pursued her and grabbed her as she got by the chaise lounger. He reached down and grabbed the pillow on the lounger with one hand while forcing her onto the floor with the other. He placed the pillow over her face and pressed, pressed harder and harder as if each push was a push for freedom from the evil that had devoured him. He was saving himself from a demon of darkness. He was not committing murder; he was freeing the world from an insidious evil that would just go on and on destroying lives. She kicked furiously until one of her high heel shoes fell off. She frantically tried to spell her killer's name with her left fingernails digging into the thick, lush carpet until she managed to carve an M. Who was the M for? Marvin Cavaletti? No, of course not, that was Sam's alias. Morton Dolton? Marvin Bolton? Martin Delman? Definitely not Mark Fitzgerald, because he was already dead. As her life ebbed away, Andy walked in and the killer, aware of someone else in the room, let go of the pillow because he knew she was dead. What could he do? Would he have to kill Andy, too? No, the chaise lounger was 6 feet long with a skirt. He tucked his knees in, scooted under it and waited.

Waiting patiently, the killer looked out from under the lounger and saw Andy's shoes at the far end. When Andy turned and went into the bedroom to call the police, the killer rolled out from under the lounger, saw the cameo broach on Mai-Mai's sweater, removed it and quickly exited the apartment. Then, of course, Andy walked back in and noticed the cameo was gone. He looked at the door and realized the killer had been in the apartment with him all the time.

Now, what occurred next is where the plot thickens and the mind of the killer becomes immersed in those dark regions that lock memories into a vault, sealing them off so the pain of remembering can be avoided. The killer was not a bad person. As the old saying goes, "there but by the graze of God goes me." All of us are capable of lapses in moral turpitude at almost anytime. There is something that can snap in all of us and we commit acts that are ordinarily out of the realm of possibility for us. The killer simply had a mind that had come unhinged for a split second, a fraction of a life-time that boiled over into mayhem caused by the pain that could no longer be endured.

The Lost Time in Private Hell 203

Every jump of the clock of destiny signalled looming calamity from the sane world by Mai-Mai's killer. The e-mails, the cell-phones and the modern conveniences of communication were not a part of the killer's life, because he lived in a solitary world where chance was the player that dealt all the cards. It was like playing solitaire with a deck of 51.

The killer was not on anyone's speed dial, so he just disappeared into the deep corridors of hopelessness where the lonely and forgotten dwell in anonymity among those poor souls who wander about blending in with their surroundings. It is the way of the modern world, where everyone is part of the crowd, but is really alone. The killer was among the living, but he did not realize that he was dead, and also those whom he saw about him were just the walking dead – people who were nothing but marionettes with strings pulled by their corporate masters. The world was a vast stage of manipulation and subterfuge. Even alcoholism was part of the corporate structure of the United States of America, where all existence fell prey to the corporate bottom line. Alcoholism was big business for the wine and spirits corporations, for the health care corporations that promised to cure what other corporations had promoted and for the pill-pushing pharmaceutical corporations that promised miracle cures through drugs that mitigated dependence on alcohol and made you dependent on some other nefarious drugs. It was a vicious cycle of control, and Mai-Mai's killer was just another poor lost soul being ground up by a society that saw people as customers, not human beings. Mai-Mai's killer had put his dastardly deed out of his conscious mind, but it was wrecking havoc with his subconscious.

He had been unceremoniously reduced to an ornamental shrub sharing the rich soil with a large and hideous tree that was crowding him out of existence. The tree of despair's long branches spread ever wider until they block out all the sunshine and joy. The killer thought he had eliminated a problem, but he had only eliminated one source of his problem. Still, fuelled by alcohol, he had created a raging bonfire of irresponsibility that let him escape into a fantasy world where he could just forget, burning to cinder the deepest of the roots of discontent, but the flames could never consume the flaws of a man who had lost his soul.

Chablis: Avenging Angel for the Forgotten
In the City of Lost Hope

Burning something down to get it back doesn't seem to make whole a lot of sense until you realize the same principle applies to nearly everything in life. The modern world is a society of the disposable – disposable diapers, disposable razor blades, disposable paper towels, even disposable morality.

The world is filled with grand buildings reaching into the sky, but there is no appreciation of that which is not grand, not large. What is wrong with small? There are grand highways crossing the country, but they all are leading people to the same place, because all along the way there are the same plastic manifestations of what is the mundane - McDonald's, Burger King, Wendy's, KFC. There is only contrived variety. Sameness is celebrated as a virtue.

Mai-Mai's killer was one of those millions who were living but had no life. He was part of a society that had conquered outer space, but had no concept of how to conquer the inner space of the people who were crying for solace in world of pain. He was just one of the many in a world filled with indifference that produced polluted souls. He was one of those characters on the computer of life and the decision makers had simply decided to hit the delete button on his existence.

This poor tortured soul wandered out of the city trying to escape the subconscious that plagued him with nightmares of something done but forgotten. He took a bus to New Jersey where one night in bar he collapsed and was hospitalized for acute alcoholism. Using the name Harold Wingate, no one knew his real name.

Strapped to a bed, he stared at the ceiling and that night came back to him. He saw what he had done. Yes, he had taken another human being's life. Did she deserve killing? Maybe so, but what gave him the right to be her executioner? Now, he was prepared to make amends. He knew someone else had been arrested for the crime. He had to do the right thing.

He started screaming wildly, ranting deliriously demanding a doctor. When the doctor came in, he tried to remain calm, because he knew an overreaction would be likely as he was going through withdrawal symptoms, and any miscalculation on his part might not allow his release so he could get to the Manhattan DA and get an innocent man out of jail. He very sedately said, "Doctor, I have to talk to you. It is important."

"My dear Mr. Wingate, I am Dr. Osborn, and I must insist that anything you want to talk about should wait until tomorrow. Right now, you are in need of sedition. You will be suffering extreme withdrawal symptoms, but we are going to take good care of you."

As Osborn motioned for the nurse to administer the hypodermic, the killer became more agitated and shouted, "It is important I get to a phone right away. You don't understand."

Osborn, seeming to be interested now, replied, "There are no telephones allowed in this ward. I'll have to get one for you." He clandestinely winked at the nurse and said, "Nurse Hampton, go tell the ward supervisor to bring a phone into room 203."

Mai-Mai's killer waited patiently as he was about to unburden his soul at long last. Then, in walked the nurse with two burly attendants and the man calling himself Harold Wingate started shouting. "I killed her, I killed her."

Osborn, very calmly replied, "It can wait, right now you need rest, complete rest. We will take care of any concerns you have tomorrow."

Again he screamed, "I killed her. I killed her. It all came back to me. I had forgotten, but it all came back to me. You have to believe me. Listen to me. Is there a condition that makes people forget, forget something bad that they did, some kind of mental disorder?"

Doctor Osborn, now holding the hypodermic, said, "There is something called Korsakoff's psychosis. It is caused by a vitamin deficiency which often is exacerbated by alcoholism. Severe

J. Wayne Frye

memory loss can result. So severe that people completely forget doing certain things. However, it can also cause confabulation where the sufferers invent memories which are then taken as true due to gaps in memory sometimes associated with blackouts. My guess is that your condition is the later. I am sure you killed no one. We can run some tests tomorrow, but now you need rest."

Life is a mosaic of possibilities, unfortunately more bad than good. We all are subject to whims of fantasy that make us think we are on the right road, but we eventually find out that we took a wrong turn somewhere along the way. That wrong turn not only has an effect on the life of the driver, but the lives of all the passengers along for the ride. The Korsakoff's psychosis suffered by Mai-Mai's killer was driving more than the killer toward a precipice. It was taking Chablis, Sam and Andy ever forward toward that deep dark abyss that waited at the end of the road of tribulations.

Korsakoff 's Psychosis Passes into the Quiet

The doctor was determined to administer the hypodermic, regardless of how much the man calling himself Harold Wingate pleaded. As the two attendants held him down while the doctor injected him with what would be the elixir that would once again confine memories of Mai-Mai's murder to the deep, dark reaches of the killer's mind, he was still pleading, but it was to no avail.

Chablis: Avenging Angel for the Forgotten
In the City of Lost Hope

The memories were once again locked in the recesses of the mind, forgotten as the man calling himself Harold Wingate, upon release a few weeks later, wandered back to Manhattan where he resumed his normal life. Still, very slowly over a period of time those memories tried to come to the surface, but could never break through. His life was altered, and he began to think that things in the past belonged in the past. There was no reason to stir the pot of discontent. Yet, he simply could not accept the cure. Something in him drove him toward the bottle. Sam McCloud, Marvin Cavaletti and many others, including the man calling himself Harold Wingate, were all victims of that devil drink which claimed so many lives and opened a Pandora's box of misery for far too many. However, there would be a seminal event which would make those memories resurface with an orgy of pain, agony and misery that would blow the lid off the case that had baffled Chablis. Korsakoff's psychosis was now at play in the field of good and evil.

The memory of what he had done faded, but deep inside he was fighting the turmoil that would not let him escape the nightmare that plagued him. How it preyed on his mind, reducing him most of the time to a snivelling whining drunk. But he simply could not understand what was plaguing him, causing him to suffer such agony. Then came the day when everything changed and the pain eased so much that he no longer was saddled with guilt. He was lifted by a ray of golden sunshine that cast a light of hope upon him. Normalcy returned and the conscious overruled the subconscious.

CHAPTER 12
FATE AWAITED THEM

Sam was leaving Chablis because he felt an impending doom and because he wanted her to accept the fact that Andy was guilty. As is so often the case when people have a fragile hold on reality, they turn to that which is so often used as medication to ease the broken spirit. Sam began his lonely journey from one bar to another. He was on his way back into despair.

You cannot lose something you do not possess, and you cannot find something you have not lost. Sam possessed nothing until he found Chablis, because he never really had Mai-Mai, so all those years trying to find that which he had never had was a search in vain. Now, as he meandered from bar to bar, using the money that he had accrued by working once again those few weeks with Chablis by his side, the demons within him were resurrected with a fury.

On the other hand, Chablis, after talking to Andy, decided that she would start the investigation anew the next day. Her immediate goal was to find Sam, and tell him that she was sorry that she let her devotion to an ideal interfere with their relationship, but that if they were going to make things work, he would have to accept her penchant for always going overboard in pursuit of justice. As a transsexual woman, she had simply encountered far too much injustice in a world that showed no real compassion. She saw suffering and had to try to cure it. She saw misery and had to try and fight it. She saw inequity and had to battle it.

Chablis had fallen for Andy because he was a red-neck working stiff who fell in love with her. She was so flattered that a man like him could actually say those words, "I love you" to a woman like her. Yet, she could always see that he was just a bit shy of total acceptance. He had never been willing to tell his family about her. He was always guarded around his friends and never stood up against their "queer joking" and singling out of those who were different. He was always careful to warn her not to tell his mother, father or brothers, as she being transgendered was just between them. She knew he was ashamed, but she endured it.

As she opened her door to leave, Andy's father and brother were standing at her door getting ready to knock. She politely said hello and said she had to go out but they could come in for a few minutes. They took a seat and she offered them coffee. Andy's father said, "No, we aren't here for pleasantries. We have heard you are seeing another man. This is absolutely unacceptable. You are Andy's wife."

Chablis, long weary of dealing with Andy's father's arrogance and uncouth behaviour said,

"Listen, you have a lot of nerve to use that tone with me. Your son was seeing Mai-Mai on the side. Where is your disdain for him?"

Sarcastically, he replied, "He is a man. That is different."

Shaking her head, Chablis replied, "Different? You think men are entitled? The days of slavery are over. Women have the same rights as men, and I am through with your son once I get him out of this jam. I am walking on the lying, cheating son-of-a-bitch."

Shocked at her directness, which she had never displayed to him before, he said, "He is a man, bitch. Men do that kind of thing. He wouldn't be much of a man if he didn't.

"They may do it Mr. Deluca, but when my man does it I am a woman who walks. You are looking at a woman who takes no shit from any man, and that includes you as well as Andy."

Andy's brother interjected, "You are acting mighty uppity woman. You better watch your mouth."

Chablis, the years of frustration dealing with the prejudicial, bigoted jerks boiling to the surface, said, "Take a hike you chauvinistic, racist, homophonic bastards. Out of my house. I don't have to put up with this any more. I did it for Andy's sake, but I am through doing it. I am going to get him out of jail, but when I do I am though with all of you thank goodness."

Mr. Deluca, said, "You are disgusting. I have even heard you have some gay friends that you flaunt in Andy's face. You are despicable."

Boiling with anger, Chablis said, "Look in your own house before you point the finger of condemnation at others. Let me tell you something. You don't know shit, asshole."

Deluca motioned for his son to get up. They both stood staring at her in disbelief. Mr. Deluca said, "My son is a real man, and I am glad he is free of a bitch like you. You aren't a woman. You are an abomination. You are a sinning bitch."

"Mr. Deluca, now you are an expert on morality? Let me tell you something. You have the morals of an alley cat. I have seen you and your pious acting wife with your crosses and Bibles lying around your house, acting holier than thou. I know what you both are. Don't call me disgusting. Your son is ashamed to tell you the truth, so here goes." At that point, Chablis, reached down, pulled up her dress and then pulled down her panties for them to see her equipment. They stood in shock, unable to speak, as she pulled her panties back up and lowered her dress.

"Now, you know the truth. I am giving you exactly 10 seconds to get out that door or I am going into the bedroom and get my 38. I'll blow so many holes in you that when you run across gay guys they will be lining up to pound one of your holes. Out. I say out!"

For the first time in the three years Chablis had known Mr. Deluca he had absolutely no retort. He was speechless. She pointed toward the door, and they turned and left. Damn, she felt good. Yeah, she was Chablis Louise Chavez and she took no prisoners. She was a woman to be reckoned with. Now, she was going to find Sam and set him straight. Tell him that he better get his ass back in her bed or she would take care of him too. She was a woman of substance, a woman who was going to rain justice down on a killer, and nothing, absolutely nothing would stop her.

Chablis was born to peasant parents who had no understanding of her affliction. They thought she was cursed and they were cursed for having her, but they were unable to see that in reality she was a special child of the God they worshipped, the very God who made her with the heart and soul of a woman who happened to be trapped in the wrong body. Her uniqueness should have made her venerated not scorned. Gender dysphoria is not a choice. It comes to special people who straddle the fence between what is and what should have been. Modern science can correct the errors of birth, but it cannot correct the ignorance of those who are locked in prejudicial ignorance. It cannot open the minds of those who adhere to a black book of cruelties called the Bible. It cannot alter governments that refuse to guarantee the rights of all and protect from harm those who are branded different and unworthy of societal approval. It cannot lift the veil of deceit practiced by those who cannot see their own callousness and insensitivity.

Chablis strolled out of her building ready to do battle. There was a certain savoir faire that made her standout as she walked out into the street in search of Sam. There was supreme confidence in her stride as her three inch heels clicked a melody of assuredness on the pavement. She was swinging her arms defiantly and men and woman alike stopped in their tracks and looked at her.

Until she met Andy, Chablis had lived her life with purpose, believing she could make a difference in the world. She had meaning to her life, but she threw it away foolishly for a buffoon who had imprisoned her for three years. She was free now.

Damn, she felt like her old self. Andy had kept her under wraps. She had been lost in a fog covering her mind. He had convinced her that only he could lead her through the fog, and only by giving into him completely could see the sunshine.

She became so compliant, so trusting that she believed she was in the sunshine. What a fool she had been.

Andy had told her she was a good listener, but he had never bothered to listen to her. She had suffered and not even realized it so accustomed she had become to Andy's control. She had always thought she was so strong, but for a brief period she let her guard down and did not protect herself. She was not true to herself for the time she was with Andy. She had refused to draw a line between him and her. Behold the rain she thought. It pours down from the heavens into a single stream clinging to individual thoughts but mixing them in the waters so they can not be distinguished. She had abrogated her individual thought. The stream takes a million drops of water and they all flow in the same direction when you are with a man like Andy. She was completely free of him now, completely free his control. Damn, how good she felt inside, and when she found Sam they would tackle the case anew, and together they would form a formable team to ensure justice was served.

The search for Sam took her to his old haunts, places he had pointed out to her by saying "Got thrown out of there. Went there and played the piano for drinks, got a job there for three weeks until they canned me. Bartender there is an easy touch, but watch out for his wife."

Chablis: Avenging Angel for the Forgotten
In the City of Lost Hope

She stopped by the Silver Bowl Bar and walked in. It was only noon, but the place was about half full, maybe 25 or 30 people, most with those glassy stares that belied the misery they were battling. This was the world where those on the margins existed. They did not live, because they had been tossed aside and forgotten by a society that had no compassion for those on the edges. America was a place where people were discarded like old worn-out shoes. Humans were disposable. When they had served their purpose, toss them aside.

She walked up to the bartender and asked if he had seen Sam McCloud or Marvin Cavaletti as he sometimes called himself.

"I remember him, McCloud that is. Ain't seen him in ages. Last time he was here had to ask him to leave."

"Any idea where he might be?"

Sighing, he said, "Just hit all the bars in the Bowery. Eventually you'll find him. Try to find ones with a piano. He likes to play you know, plays for drinks."

Chablis went to bar after bar and always the same. He had been in the Silver Slipper only a few hours earlier. He had played the piano there for awhile until the tips dried up and along with them the drinks.

It was easy for Chablis to get help, as the bartenders were pleased to talk to such a beautiful woman. One suggested she go to work for him, but no Sam anywhere.

Chablis gave up around 10:00 PM, figuring that tomorrow was another day. Surely she could find him then. She began to stroll somewhat aimlessly but for some reason she wound up on Park Avenue.

A loving soul like Chablis is always yearning, always searching. She moves ever forward to find that which is lost be it a person, an object or an idea. Her eyes are always gazing toward that serenity, hope, promise and justice that is just over the hill. Hope is never lost within her, because it abides in a heart of gold where the treasure is stored in goodness, graciousness and kindness. She longs to bring peace to those who have none. As long as tears flow from the afflicted of mind, body and spirit like benevolent rain dropping into a stream of faithful expectation she moves with the assuredness of a dedicated soldier in the battle against adversity. As the water of misery overflows it banks and tumultuously sweeps the forgotten toward annihilation, she stands as a bulwark to stem the flow. When the barren highways lead to closed gates of fairness among the ruins perpetrated by the uncaring, this daughter of hope rises from the depths to slay catastrophe and calamity. Pure tears of empathy flow from this daughter of resilience, hope and promise. Dewdrops of concern form at her feet in silent homage to a woman whose devotion to the forgotten sanctifies her. She was in search of justice for him who betrayed her, but that was the mark upon her brow that glorified her goodness. And her kind heart beat with the rhythm of concern for her dear Sam, who had to battle the demons of alcohol. His was a lonely battle, and she longed to be by his side to steady him. She was a Goddess of devotion to those who were forgotten in the city of lost hope.

She suddenly came to a stop in front of a shop. She leaned against the shop window that from behind the safety grating displayed expensive silver candelabras, wine cisterns, monogrammed serving trays and other items reserved for those who were at the top of the social strata. Yes, she was in front of the shop where Sam had stood the night of the murder. She, like Sam had, reflected on the cameo he had bought Mai-Mai on her birthday. She reached up and rubbed the little scar on her forehead with her index finger as she thought. Sam had called it a little scar of love that seemed to long for a delicate kiss of thankfulness from a man who had been lost but was now found. But where was he thought Chablis, as she looked over at the Cavaletti Building.

Chablis: Avenging Angel for the Forgotten
In the City of Lost Hope

Like Sam, on that faithful night when he stood there, she began to shiver, not from the cold, but from fear of something that waited to close the veil of misery upon her. She needed to find Sam. She looked to her right and there was the bar Sam had gone into that night when Mai-Mai met her demise. It was the place where he found two kind souls who tried to satisfy his over-powering need for a drink. Sure thought Chablis, it wasn't likely he would be in an uptown bar, but why not take a look. What could it hurt?

It wasn't a nice place by the standards of Park Avenue, but the people there were definitely upper middle class, except for one dishevelled looking man sitting at a table in the back of the bar. Chablis strolled over to him.

The man seemed to be whimpering. His hair was uncombed, his clothes looked like he had slept in them and he appeared to have two or three days growth of beard. She placed her hand on his shoulder and said, "Hi there Sam."

Sam wiped his brow, raised his head and tears began to flow. She sat down beside him and said, "It's OK, darling. You walked out on me. I didn't walk out on you. Come on home, and we will deal with this."

Sam, his tears drying, replied, "I don't deserve the love of a woman like you."

Chablis, smiling that gorgeous smile that lights up a room, replied, "Of course you don't silly, but you have it anyway."

They laughed together and the world around them seemed at peace. All was right and the pain Sam felt seemed to dissipate as he said, "Thank you for loving me, darling. I am so sorry, but I so want you to cling to me. I should be your rock upon which you can lean, rather than the other way around. I am with you sweetheart 100%, and we will find Mai-Mai's killer and free Andy. Take me home and I'll bathe, put the demon of alcohol behind me again, and we will start out fresh tomorrow morning in pursuit of Mai-Mai's killer."

Chablis smiled, helped the unstable Sam up by holding his right side to steady him and they started to walk slowly and deliberately toward the door. Little did the lovers know that an ill fate awaited them?

EPILOGUE
I KILLED MAI-MAI

Life is a circuitous road,
not a straight thoroughfare.
We shall not cease from the search for truth.
Yet, the end of all our searching will be to
arrive where we started the search
and know the place for the first time.
After the end is before the end.

On the way out, Sam and Chablis passed by a table where a middle aged blond and an elderly man were sitting. It was the kind woman who had befriended Sam that night when he reached into his coat pocket and gave her a present. The woman looked up at Sam and smiled. "Hi there friend. Haven't seen you since that night you reached in your pocket and gave me this beautiful broach," she said as she fingered Mai-Mai's cameo which was pinned to her chest.

Sam looked at Chablis and nearly collapsed as he unsteadily eased into a chair next to the woman, never taking his eyes off the broach. Tears flowed down Chablis face as Sam uttered, "I had Korsakoff's psychosis. I killed Mai-Mai!"

Chablis: Avenging Angel for the Forgotten
In the City of Lost Hope